About the Author

Clare O'Dea is originally from Dublin and has lived in Switzerland since 2003. After studying French and Russian at Trinity College Dublin, she went on to have a varied media career in Ireland and Switzerland, with a freelance stint in Russia. Her first non-fiction book, *The Naked Swiss: A Nation Behind 10 Myths*, was published in 2016. Clare turned to Ireland as a subject for her second book, *The Naked Irish: Portrait of a Nation Beyond the Clichés* (2019). *Voting Day* is her debut fiction book.

https://clareodea.com

Voting Day

CLARE O'DEA

Fairlight Books

First published by Fairlight Books 2022

Fairlight Books
Summertown Pavilion, 18–24 Middle Way, Oxford, OX2 7LG

A CIP catalogue record for this book is available from the
British Library

1 2 3 4 5 6 7 8 9 10

ISBN 978-1-914148-07-1

www.fairlightbooks.com

Printed and bound in Great Britain by Clays Ltd.

Designed by Sara Wood

Illustrated by Sam Kalda

This is a work of fiction. Names, characters, business, events
and incidents are the products of the author's imagination.
Any resemblance to actual persons, living or dead, or actual
events is purely coincidental.

MIX
Paper from
responsible sources
FSC® C018072

For the women who paved the way

Every era has its favourite illusions, and one of the most cherished of our century is that of 'the modern woman', the professionally equal, independent and successful woman.

—Iris von Roten, *Frauen im Laufgitter* (1958)

Part I

Vreni

It was going to be the best possible day. Vreni didn't care about the fog that had been smothering the farm since Friday; she didn't care about the sandwiches for the vote or the milk jug broken by the foster boy. In a few hours she would be walking around Bern arm in arm with her daughter, Margrit, admiring the sights, going for coffee and cake. For now, she had the warm kitchen to herself and the pile of potatoes getting steadily smaller as she worked the grater at flying speed. Vreni was renowned for her rösti.

The story of the girl who spun straw into gold came to mind and she smiled. When did she first hear that? In third class probably, from Sister Jerome with her funny French accent. A prince held the girl captive, forcing her to keep spinning more gold, and wasn't there an old witch who helped with her magic? But then she wanted something in return. It was usually the firstborn child in these stories. The faintest memory of Vreni's first labour twenty-three years earlier made its way towards her then, like a wisp of drifting smoke. She certainly wasn't going to think about that! So she summoned an image of her open suitcase instead – beautifully packed. The new toilet bag with all her bits and bobs. Her best cardigan to wear in hospital. Why not? These were city people, and she didn't want to be treated like some kind of rough *Oberländerin* who hardly felt pain.

She got up and put the pan on to heat. Best to concentrate on the here and now. Yes, let the family have a nice breakfast. She'd even send little Ruedi out to the henhouse for a few eggs. They would get their Sunday breakfast out of her today and nothing else for six weeks. Six whole weeks. She would have it in writing, Dr Jungo had promised.

The clock struck the half hour. They would all be up soon, her three sons shuffling into the kitchen with their identical snub noses (a seemingly unshakeable legacy from Peter's side of the family) and their big feet; Peter claiming the head of the table, probably still sulking about the sandwiches fight, and little Ruedi, hopelessly timid and as clumsy as the day he arrived. So exasperating. She should have stuck to her guns and got a girl this time. A girl would come in useful now.

She finished the last potato and sprinkled some nutmeg, salt and pepper into the bowl. Bracing herself, she carried the bowl over to the stove and set it down. Then she reached for the kettle. Why did everything have to be so heavy? In the kitchens of the future, which she'd seen with her own eyes at the Saffa fair in Zurich, they would have light plastic versions of everything instead of all this dead weight, and she would be first in line.

The fat sizzled in the pan. Vreni transferred the grated potato to the pan and grabbed a cloth to wipe the table. She cleared the potato peels into the scraps bucket. Though the days were getting ever so slightly longer, dawn was still more than an hour off, and the black night still pressed against the steamed-up windows. How many winter mornings had she spent in here baking, cleaning, pot-walloping? Thousands.

At the farm, one week blurred into the next as nature crawled predictably from season to season. Always so much to do. Sunrises and sunsets to beat the band – very pretty and everything, but she felt like she had seen all the variations. Later today she would be walking on a footpath and waiting for traffic to pass before crossing the street between houses so tall you could not see their roofs. The relief of seeing so many different faces and being sure not to recognise a single one. People wearing well-cut clothes, and Margrit and her walking along happily through the crowd. Vreni balled her fists and clenched them close to her face, indulging in a little convulsion of excitement. That set off the godawful dragging feeling down below. So she did her pelvic floor exercises while she patted the potato down nice and firm.

Whatever happened, Vreni was not going to make the sandwiches. She didn't even realise it had become a tradition until it was too late. That's the problem with doing a favour. You offer to do a kind act once and that's fine. But do it a second time and you might find yourself locked into an obligation for life, especially with this husband of hers.

Peter liked to be involved in things. He was on the commune council and said yes to every committee going. Currently that meant a seat on the Poor Committee, the Roads Committee, the Graveyard Committee and the Voting Day Committee. They all came in useful, but voting was his favourite. People came in from all over on voting day. There were faces that wouldn't be seen any other time apart from the moving of the herds twice a year. It was the best time to exchange a few words with men from every corner of the commune. News was extracted about who was selling fields and animals, who had found work where, who needed extra hands or had sons or daughters looking for work. He would spend the whole day flitting around the commune administration office, mostly at the desk greeting voters, sometimes waylaying an old hunting buddy at the entrance. He would even grit the snow on the path outside if needed. After the ballot box was collected, he would return home in the late afternoon, triumphant and flushed from the schnapps they always had to round off a good day of democracy. The family would eat a late dinner while he entertained them all with the best nuggets of news.

And on voting day, Vreni always made sandwiches for the men who were manning the ballot boxes. Apparently she was renowned for her sandwiches, too, made with *Zopf* bread, fresh butter, generous slices of ham and a smear of mustard. Lord, what a fuss they made about those sandwiches even though there was no secret to them whatsoever! A toddler could make them and her fifty-two-year-old husband would make them this morning with her fresh bread before she boarded the bus and coasted down the valley away from it all. No ifs or buts.

The door of the little box room off the kitchen opened and a ten-year-old boy with tousled blond hair stood on the threshold. She never had to wake Ruedi. He always appeared at the right moment, already dressed, as if he could sense when she was ready for him. Some kind of survival instinct picked up at the Home, she imagined.

'Good morning, Frau Sutter,' he said in that musical way of his. That's one thing she noticed about him: he had a sweet voice, like a flute. Hard to believe what a bad family he came from – the father a drunk and the mother from one of those gypsy clans. He was lucky to be placed with a good family, but there is only so much you can do with cases like that. Nature will out, she'd seen it enough times.

'Put your boots on there, lad, and go and get me however many eggs you can find.'

Ruedi got ready but hovered at the back door. He pulled at the sleeve of his sweater exactly as she'd told him not to. His lips were pursed as if he had something to say.

'What is it?'

'You... you're going to hospital today.' Such a visible effort to get out a few words.

'That's right. I'll be back in three weeks. I told you already.' She turned back to the stove.

'But.'

'What?'

'Hospital is dangerous. Maybe you shouldn't go.'

'Come here,' Vreni said, setting down the wooden spoon.

He looked down at his boots, afraid to step on the clean floor. Vreni went to him.

'What makes you think hospitals are dangerous?'

He pulled harder on his cuff and Vreni was sure she'd need to darn it again soon. 'My friend at the

Home, Dänu. He went to hospital and he...' Ruedi's eyes brimmed with tears.

Vreni had an urge to pull him into her arms, but she didn't feel it was her place. He was not a baby. But he was someone else's baby. With a twinge of guilt, she thought of the unanswered letters in her drawer. So carefully written, the same appeal every time.

She patted his shoulder. 'I'm sorry about your friend. But don't worry about me. People go to hospital all the time to get things fixed, and they come home again feeling better. It will be the same with me and my hip. Now what about those eggs? It's a special breakfast today.'

Ruedi compressed his lips and nodded his head. How little she knew about him really.

Vreni went back to the rösti which was beautifully golden-brown underneath. The hip story worked well, even with her own boys. Where were those sons of hers? She needed someone to turn out the rösti onto the big platter, quickly before it burned. And the bread was nearly done. Vreni turned on the radio and cranked it up loud. A bit of accordion would do the trick.

Hugo appeared a minute later, wearing a woollen sweater over his night clothes. He went straight for the radio and snapped it off. 'They're coming,' he said. She assumed he had a hangover, based on the late hour he had rolled in at the night before and his loud preparations for bed. And what harm? He needed to let off steam with his friends after three weeks in the army barracks.

'Put this out on the plate for me,' Vreni answered, turning the pan handle towards him. 'We've a lot to get through this morning.'

Ruedi materialised at her elbow, offering a basket of eggs. Vreni shivered. He'd brought the cold in with him.

'Stick them there on the counter and start setting the table. And be careful with the crockery!'

While Vreni fried the eggs and filled the coffee pot, Marcel and Ueli came in and joined their brother at the table. The three boys were all the same size now, built wide and not too tall like their father. They sat slumped in their places staring at the upended golden rösti, ignoring Ruedi who put the plates, mugs and cutlery in front of them. Vreni distributed the fried eggs over the potato dish and took her place, back to the window. Where the hell was Peter?

Just as Vreni was about to lose her cool – not in a loud way of course, more like an underground explosion – Peter made his entrance and greeted the family with 'Morning, all.' They all joined hands and said grace. 'For food and drink, for our daily bread, we thank you, oh God.'

The bread! Vreni moved at her top speed towards the oven, which wasn't fast at all. She hauled out the loaves, which were a shade darker than she would have liked, and placed the tray on the stove top.

'Come and serve, Vreni,' Peter said. Hot now, and devilishly uncomfortable with her symptoms, Vreni went and served the men one by one, Ruedi last. Marcel poured the coffee and gave her a look of understanding when she reached her cup out towards him. But what did he understand? Nothing, that's what.

'Today's a big day for Ueli,' Peter clapped his eldest son on the back. 'You two will have to hold the fort.' He pointed his fork at Hugo and Marcel. Ueli sat up straighter and showed off all his twenty-one years.

'What time should I come down to vote, Papi?'

'A big day indeed.' The head of the household looked around the table for approval. 'My eldest son, a grown man, voting today for the first time. I remember my first voting day—'

'I'm going to interrupt you there.' Vreni wasn't having this. She had a busier morning than anyone today and she didn't have time for political speeches. But Marcel began talking over them both.

'Well, Ueli, will you be doing the right thing by your mother today?' her youngest asked. 'So she can go with you next time?'

Ueli looked to his father.

'He'll be doing the right thing for his country, a country that has been well ruled by decent men for seven hundred years. The envy of Europe.' Peter held Ueli's gaze.

'More like the embarrassment of Europe,' Marcel retorted, his cheeks flushed with indignation. 'Are Swiss women not as clever as French women – or German women or Austrian women for that matter?'

'Nonsense,' Peter mumbled through a mouthful of potato and egg. 'Cheeky gymnasium pup – Swiss women are better looked after than any of that lot and well you know it.'

'Thank you, everyone, but I've got more important things to talk about,' Vreni said, and she took her list out of her apron pocket. 'Just eat up and listen.'

*

Her cousin's girl was due to arrive after lunch so Vreni wouldn't get to do the handover in person, but she had everything written out, pages of instructions. What was in the basement stores, what to cook each day of the week, what provisions were needed from the village shop and what day to buy them, what clothes to wash and when, in what order to clean the rooms of the house. Ruedi was taking over her outside jobs, mercifully fewer and lighter in winter. She had no idea how handy this girl was, but she had her concerns about the child's physique.

Last time she'd seen her was at her mother's funeral three years ago, when she'd been very scrawny for a fourteen-year-old. Hopefully she'd filled out by now. Anyway, beggars can't be choosers. She was lucky to find a body to replace her and lucky to get the help so cheap. Her cousin Christina, Lord rest her, had run a good house and would surely have passed on the essentials. Everything would be fine.

Vreni had written down everything the doctor suggested she bring. When it was time to get ready, she went to check her case one last time and put the hospital letter in her handbag. It still said the same thing: 'Please present yourself at reception at 5pm Sunday 01.02.59 to be ready for your operation on Monday 2nd. Nil by mouth from 5pm on the 1st.' Everything was in order, and she sat down on the bed for a little relief from the constant aching. Her hat and good coat were laid out beside her, ready.

A strange current of nerves ran through her body, catching in her chest, and she tried to breathe it away. Ever since Dr Jungo had told her what was ailing her, she had been determined to go for the operation. Only a full cure would do. The more she thought about it, the more excited she got and there wasn't room for fear most of the time. A few days of pain would be nothing compared to the years of dis-comfort behind her. Rest was the word that jumped out at her when he explained the ins and outs. She was giddy about the prospect of rest. She would be looked after, two weeks in hospital and one week in the convalescent home. People would bring her food and cups of tea, change the sheets and provide hot water, and when she came home, she would be unavailable. And to top it all she had managed to swing this day with Margrit on the way to the hospital. Peter was too busy to accompany her today; it couldn't be more perfect.

With a few minutes to spare, Vreni went back into the kitchen and took pity on Peter, who was actually making the sandwiches with the skill of a toddler. She took over the buttering and left him on ham-slicing duty.

'Are you all right?' he asked her. 'Ready for tomorrow?' She thought she detected an echo of tenderness in his voice.

'I'll be fine,' she said. 'They do these operations every day of the week. It's nothing complicated, Dr Jungo said' – she caught herself – 'but still serious, and rest is very important for the recovery. He was very insistent on that.'

'Yes, so you keep saying. Well, I'll telephone the clinic tomorrow afternoon for news.' He went over to the dresser and took out his wallet. 'Here, for the train ticket and maybe you'll want to buy some fruit or a magazine.'

Vreni accepted the ten-franc note. Her suitcase was waiting by the door.

'Let's go down together,' she said. 'I'll get my coat.'

The boys came out of the shed to wish her well. Hugo tried to get away with a peck on the cheek, but she got a grip of his upper arm and placed her other hand on his face.

'Safe journey back this evening and don't be late again. You don't want to have to wait another three weeks to come home, do you?' He shrugged in response. 'You know you could send me a letter in Bern,' she went on, 'care of the Women's Hospital. Something to do on one of those boring evenings at the barracks.

'Look at his face,' she said to the others. 'As if I'd asked him to embroider a cushion for me!' Hugo had an entire repertoire of sullen looks and she wasn't sure if she'd gone too far. The Sutters did not respond well to teasing. She winked at him.

Vreni got a half embrace from Ueli and a proper hug from Marcel. Ruedi hung back in the shadows of the pig shed and gave a little wave when she looked his way. She mouthed 'don't worry' at him.

'Be good,' she called to them all, suddenly gripped with impatience to leave. 'And no bad language around your cousin.' The bus was due in forty minutes, just before the community building opened for voting at nine. Husband and wife set off down the lane followed by the dog.

With the orchard to their left, they walked through the dense fog, Peter carrying the suitcase and basket of sandwiches. The farmhouse and out-buildings quickly vanished behind them. Along the top field they walked, the one they had planted with beet and cabbage just before the ground turned hard last autumn. A beautiful field when you could see it, wide and fertile, sweeping down to the river, taking up half the hillside. Having grown up around much thinner topsoil higher up the valley, Vreni still appreciated the good land around the village. The dog stopped in his usual lookout place, but he wouldn't see much today. He adopted his watching stance anyway, as if he was too proud to admit it had been a wasted journey. Vreni smiled.

The ground was pockmarked with stiff peaks and hollows, and frozen puddles cracked underfoot as they walked. Vreni sought out the panes of ice; it was a pleasing sound. Otherwise, both were silent, each with their own thing to look forward to. Vreni couldn't wait to see Margrit with her lovely com-plexion and sparkling eyes. The fog appeared to part before them as they walked, opening up a narrow corridor of visibility and closing again behind them. As if they were alone in the world. What proof did she have that their home and the village were really there? Vreni thought of something deep to say about how this walk in the fog was like life or marriage – but Peter wasn't the right audience, for this or most of her thoughts, so she left it.

They took the straight path through the wood. The aching and dragging grew stronger and with it came a stab of mental anguish, worse than the physical discomfort. The indignity of her womb pushing its way down. You want out, I'll get you out!

Dr Jungo said her particular problem was very common in this part of the country. He had written to the newspaper about it. Families were large and the farmers' wives worked too late into pregnancy and returned to normal duties too quickly after childbirth. The houses were so scattered that there was little opportunity for solidarity among neighbour women, and the mothers' own families, their first families, were too far away to help.

Vreni was sure she had done the most damage when Peter was away on active duty during the war. Even with two young lads from the orphanage living in and the older Sutter relatives giving a half day here and there, she'd never had enough help for the farm work and the house. She'd tied Hugo in a sling and taken him everywhere with her. Two years later the same with Marcel. The rest of the time, the poor children spent far too many hours in the playpen.

She hardly played with them at all compared to the attention Margrit and Ueli had got. And then all those winter evenings with no one to talk to and the blackout blinds hemming her in. She'd thought she might die of loneliness. The children represented work to her, not company. No, that wasn't fair, Margrit was entertaining with her cheerful patter and all her questions about the world.

She remembered Margrit sharing the bed with her; she would have been six or seven. When the baby cried at night, Vreni was sometimes too dead tired to move. Margrit would climb over her prostrate mother, pick the infant up from his cradle and haul him into position in the valley between them both so he could get a little comfort at Vreni's breast. She was always kind, that girl, and full of affection. Vreni was so glad to start the family with a girl, it set the tone for the younger children. Much less rough and tumble.

The peace of the forest was disturbed by the sound of hooves breaking frosty twigs – the chamois herd. They must be close to the spot where Peter left hay out for the animals. Vreni automatically checked her mental food inventory. They still had a few cuts of cured meat in the basement from the old doe he had killed in October. She should have put game stew on the list for Christina's daughter.

'How much longer do you think Margrit will keep up this life in town?' Peter said out of the blue.

'What do you mean?' Vreni knew what he meant, but was used to pretending not to when the subject of Margrit came up.

'You know what I mean, the job, the tiny attic room, those smoky streets. She stands to lose her looks. And the men are not suitable in the city, stuck-up pen pushers with wandering hands. If she came to see us more often, she might get some offers around here.'

'She doesn't want this life, Peter. She's a modern woman with everything open to her. She's got her bookkeeping certificate, which hopefully she'll soon get to use. Why would she want to hoe the rows and feed pigs all day in the back of beyond when she can sit in a nice warm office?' The cold was pinching Vreni's fingers at that moment in a cruel grip.

'It doesn't have to be a farm. The village is full of young men, and most of the girls are off working as maids. She could have her pick. What about the Schwaller lad she used to pal around with?'

'Margrit's not going to be a cheesemaker's wife, Peter. Don't you remember, she used to cross the road to avoid the smell there?' She started to laugh. 'The only Swiss child who ever hated cheese... honestly, Peter!' Her husband paused and set down his load. He was shaking. They caught each other's eye and that set their mirth free. Vreni had tears in her eyes; she couldn't stop. Peter's honking set her off every time her chugging laugh subsided.

He reached out and took her hand in his and that calmed them both. 'Let's say our goodbyes here, pet,' he said. Her chin fitted on his shoulder and she gripped his bulk firmly. 'You'll be good as new again soon.'

'That's the plan.' Did he remember the two of them coming to this forest when they were courting? Lord, the passion they'd had for each other! She was helping out over at the Meyers' place while the mother had trouble with her nerves, and they met here all through the summer and into the autumn. Talk about wandering hands! It was glorious.

'I just worry that she's grown so far apart from us.' The spell was broken and Peter scooped up the bags again. 'If Aunt Marta hadn't singled her out like that...' He shook his head.

'Well, it was the proudest day of my life when she got into commercial college, and I'll be forever grateful to your aunt, Lord rest her, for making that possible.' Vreni could answer without thinking, so often had they had this exchange with each other. Good old Aunt Marta, she paid for one daughter from each of her siblings' families to get training in whatever they were good at. Seven cousins scattered over the highlands and beyond all got a good start thanks to her. With their confidence and earning power, each was the envy of their brothers and sisters.

The village church bells pealed as if to remind them that the outside world was waiting. Peter always skipped Mass on voting Sundays, and Margrit considered she had special dispensation today. She could always say a prayer in the hospital chapel tonight. She'd even heard the priest came around on Sundays to give the Host to patients too ill to get up. It seemed terribly glamorous and she had her heart set on having this experience.

When they came out the other side of the forest, the fog was thinning, and they could see all the way to the road running parallel to their path fifty metres to the left. The muffled noise of a car engine was followed by two meagre headlight beams and then a car, which was hardly going much faster than them.

'The bus will be terribly slow today. I hope you don't miss your train.'

Vreni spontaneously quickened her pace, as if that would make any difference. The prospect of missing the train struck her as a catastrophe. She was so looking forward to seeing Margrit. Their time together would be halved. Would Margrit even have the sense to wait for her? She might think her mother wasn't coming after all. She might go back to her lodgings to look for a message. She would be confused and come back to the station irritable. She would be cold. She would have to buy a sandwich at the station buffet and eat on her own. And all the time Vreni would be waiting in the shelter at her local station, freezing gradually from the toes up, not a single place open where she could get so much as a glass of water.

She bowed her head and stuffed one hand in each sleeve like a monk. 'I won't miss the train, even if I have to whip the bus driver all the way to the station.'

Peter grinned. 'I wouldn't put it past you.'

They parted opposite the church, and Vreni took her place on the bus-stop bench inside the new shelter. Her husband had been part of the committee that had put in the bench and shelter two years before. It was either that or a Lourdes grotto and thankfully the side of reason won. The grotto campaigners took the loss hard and they weren't giving up. The last thing she heard there was a petition going around. Well, she liked a nice grotto as much as the next person, but at this particular moment the bench was worth its weight in gold.

From the direction of the church came a huddled figure walking briskly with a slight limp. It was the last person Vreni wanted to see. Could she be getting the bus, too? How would Vreni get out of the interrogation? She fished around in her pockets for a handkerchief and dabbed her nose. She did a trial cough to see how authentic it sounded. Not very. Anna Sturny raised her hand in greeting from the other side of the road and made a beeline for her.

'Greetings to you, Vreni.' Anna's cheeks were as red as a teething baby's. 'Terrible fog today.'

'Hello, Anna, terrible weather indeed.'

'They say it will clear up mid-morning.'

'Is that right?'

Anna sat down next to her, a little too close. So she was getting the bus, too. Vreni coughed and did a convincing job of blowing her nose, which was actually in need of mopping after the effort of the walk. She edged away from Anna. 'I don't want to give you my cold.'

'Oh don't worry, I never catch anything,' Anna said. 'Did all my sickness in one go as a young girl.' She patted her polio-affected leg. 'Paid my dues then.'

Vreni needed a topic quickly before the questions started. What could they talk about? Of course! The men. Anna loved to talk about her husband.

'Peter's just gone off to look after the vote. Is Samuel around?'

'He has to visit his mother first. We got word she'd had a bad night. Samu rushed down to see if there was anything he could do. He's asked me to get a special tea for her chest and her dizziness so that's where I'm off to now. My cousin Kathrin in Plasselb has the most amazing herbal mixes – well, you must know that. Poor Samu, he wants to feel like he's doing something. He already has the doctor booked and paid for to come once a week.

He's very attached to his mother. Do anything for her.'

'Except give her the vote.'

Vreni did not know what had come over her. She wasn't one for smart remarks, at least not out loud. And the vote was the last thing on her mind. What did she care how Samuel voted? The man was a buffoon. She didn't expect her own son or husband to vote yes to the women's vote. The system worked well and women didn't know enough about politics. She didn't mind, it was Marcel who minded and he was so young.

Anna was staring at her, perplexed. Her cheeks turned a shade redder. She opened and closed her mouth twice.

'Samuel's mother is bedridden and can hardly speak since the stroke. What would she want with the vote? Don't tell me you want *us* to be bored to death with politics, too? Haven't we enough to worry about?'

'I'm sorry, Anna. I didn't mean it. Just a bad joke. I'm sorry for Frau Sturny. Oh look, the bus is here!'

The fog was definitely clearing. As she watched the bus turn, Vreni could see down the street all the way to the grocers. They could still leave on time if the driver was willing to forgo his break. She had to make that train.

Anna's eyes narrowed as Vreni pulled the suit-case towards her. The game was up.

'I never asked you where you were going, Vreni. Off to see the world, is it?'

'You know me, always on the move. This time it's a cruise on the Nile.' Vreni gave a tight smile.

'But you're going somewhere alone, with a suit-case, on a Sunday?' Anna wasn't giving up that easily. They both took a step forward as the bus approached. So he was keeping to the timetable, good man. 'You can tell me all about it on the bus,' Anna said, and Vreni's heart sank.

Vreni tried to be vague, playing things down as much as possible. It would be silly to deny that she was going to hospital now, because everyone would know by the time she got back. But Anna was better than Hercule Poirot himself. In the ten minutes it took them to get to the next village, she had, question by question, worn Vreni down until she revealed the truth. She left with an unasked-for promise to order special teas from her cousin.

That's that, thought Vreni, the cat's out of the bag. It shouldn't matter that people would find out her business, it wasn't a scandal, but she hated the idea of being talked about or, even worse, pitied. And she didn't want anyone thinking about her body in any way. That was part of it, too.

After Anna got off the bus, there was nobody else Vreni recognised among the other passengers. She looked out the window and settled into her own thoughts as the dull countryside emerged from the lifting fog. It was a scene badly in need of a fresh dressing of snow: muddy lanes leading to shabby houses, bare trees and fields drained of life and colour.

She wondered if everyone at this stage of life felt the same crushing tedium that came with the realisation that this was it, there would be no meaningful change. She had chosen her man, her home, her corner of the world and everything that came with it. How would she pass the time for the next twenty or thirty years until she was bedridden like old Frau Sturny? Certainly not like the characters in her English detective stories who wore evening gowns and drank cocktails and played tennis! More likely in and around the house and, when she met neighbours in the village, talking about other people's children and sick elderly relatives for the rest of her life.

The bus passed the brand-new AMAG car showroom, which looked like something out of California, or what Vreni imagined California to be like. Hugo had finished his bricklayer's apprenticeship working on that building, before he went off to do his military service. The last time she had come this way it had been a shell. Now, the white building had two curved wings with full-length windows. To think that her son had contributed to such an impressive project. Soon it would be full of cars from all over the world. Peter had talked about finally buying a car this summer. It had to be new and it had to be American, and he had insisted on waiting as long as it took to save up the full amount. Maybe having a car would make a difference. He could bring her on drives, they'd visit some castles or lakes. Surely they would visit Margrit more often, too.

As the bus got closer to town, she noticed one building site after another, some obviously industrial, or was that a supermarket she just saw? She twisted around in her seat to look. It was a whole new neighbourhood, with apartment buildings that looked big enough for four or six or ten families. Where were all these people going to come from? She had the feeling Switzerland had been changing behind her back. Or maybe there were two Switzerlands and she had ended up in the wrong one.

When had she last taken the bus to town, a mere forty-minute journey? Peter went often enough to the bank or the farmers' co-op or on commune business, and she sometimes asked him to get something specific from the haberdashery or the stationer's. They bought most of their clothes from the catalogue. Could it be that she hadn't left the village since the trip to the Saffa exhibition in Zurich last August? Goodness, how small her life had become.

That had been a heady day. Half the village went – the women, that is. The women's association rented a bus, and they left at six in the morning and got to Zurich by eleven. It was the most extravagant thing most of them had ever done and was very much driven by the only person from Zurich in the village, Maria Schär, who saw her chance and took it.

The exhibition of women and work was spread over a huge space on the lake shore. Vreni lost the others in the crowd pretty quickly and half deliberately, and wandered from stand to stand in a state of delight. She especially loved the pretend sitting rooms they had done up with modern furniture and fittings. And the kitchens with all the plastic implements and containers. She still remembered the English word for plastic – Tupperware. The section on women's jobs was less interesting, but the highlight was in the middle of the afternoon when she came upon an all-female string quartet playing in the open air. She ate an ice cream as she strolled, and the effect of the music and the lake view and the feeling that she had been transported to a world just for women was quite magical. Vreni was glad to find her gang from the village again at the rendezvous and see the same flush of happiness in their cheeks. She felt they had witnessed something special together and that things might be different somehow from then on. And then, instead of joining the women's association, as Anna had been pestering her to do for years, or asking Peter for a proper allowance or planting a flower garden or getting a book about Ancient Rome or making a trip to the National Historical Museum, all ideas she had had on the way home from Zurich, she had sat at home for the rest of the year, and buried herself in her routine. The only engagements she'd had this winter were doctor's appointments.

And the funny thing was that, before she was ever known for her sandwiches, and perhaps her unfriendliness, she used to be known for her bright personality. She was the lively one in the family, the one with the biggest laugh. She was interested in people and stories and fashion. She used to collect pictures from magazines and draw her own clothes designs. Somewhere along the way she had got the idea that she was special (the teachers praised her so!), and that her life might be different from her cousins' and neighbours' lives in some way, that she would perhaps be discovered by an important person and that interesting things would happen.

Yet there was no mysterious benefactor and, after seven years as a maid in three different households, that feeling of being special was starting to give way to a feeling of panic. So when she was offered a live-in waitressing job at the Alpenrose Hotel in town, she did not feel lucky. On the contrary, Vreni had a sudden fear of being doomed to serve at other people's tables for life and never her own. She had been in a few scary situations with unpleasant men. She needed a way out. The grim realisation dawned that there was an acceptable amount of time for a young girl to try to make her way without much progress and she was reaching the end of that phase.

And then she met Peter again, the young pig farmer who had charmed his way into her underwear that summer when she was living with the Meyers. He came to her uncle's funeral and he was delighted to see her – delighted. It was the first time she had seen him in a suit, and it made a difference. Though the farm was only twelve miles away from her home on the edge of a village of four hundred souls, it was a step up, as her mother pointed out. It turned out her life was not going to be different or special, but it would be secure. And, it must be said, he really seemed pleased with the catch. He felt lucky. A good start in marriage for any woman. It set the tone.

The bus pulled in alongside the station, and Vreni thanked the driver and descended the steps gingerly. The town, free of fog, was looking its usual charmless self. All the greys of man and nature were represented. From the station you could see the co-op building with its grain tower, the metalworks, the municipal buildings and the old Alpenrose Hotel.

The main shopping street descended to her right on the way to the Catholic church, the post office and the new cinema. The Protestant church and the new secondary school her children had attended were in the parallel street. They liked it here, but it had never been her town. Standing still for even a minute, the cold was quick to find her. It snaked up under her skirt and around the back of her neck. Her eyes began to water. Maybe it wasn't such a great day for sightseeing. Never mind, she could spend the whole time in a tea room with Margrit, and she'd be happy.

Vreni bought her ticket at the outdoor counter and made straight for the closed shelter on the main platform. She greeted the other passengers waiting inside, two men and a woman, and received the obligatory response but was pleased to note their total lack of curiosity about her. All the better.

Thirty-five minutes is quite a wait in an unheated room on a Swiss train platform in February. Vreni had the dual challenge of urgently needing to use the facilities while also being fiercely thirsty. The strong coffee and salty rösti combination was making itself felt, but she couldn't bring herself to get up in front of these people and traipse back down to the other end of the platform so publicly. She resolved to wait for the train.

Through the glass she could see a poster featuring a pretty young girl with her hair in a nice chignon.

The poster caption read, 'Leave us out of the game', and the girl held up her gloved palm towards the camera lens making the gesture 'stop'. Plenty of serious, important people thought women shouldn't have the vote. They seemed to know what they were talking about. Vreni didn't mind for herself, but when she thought about the younger generation, was it fair for her sons to be able to vote and not her daughter? Margrit was cleverer than Hugo and Ueli put together. That hairstyle would look nice on Margrit, she thought, though she wore her hair a bit too short now for it to work.

Margrit had style, something that pleased her mother no end. She had the knack for finding the right cut or colour and creating nice outfits with small touches. Clothes that might look common-place on another girl looked handmade for her. She also had a great shape, filling her clothes in the right places. Vreni got a lot of pleasure from just watching her daughter move around the place. She had a sort of magnetism which Vreni saw other people affected by too, not just her, though her response to her daughter's physical presence was shot through with pride as well as admiration. What Margrit had, Vreni suspected she had once had as well. It was something you sometimes saw in girls or young women, an intersection of good health and youth and beauty that peaked at a certain point in time, when they positively shone, and some people could hardly make eye contact with them because of it. Margrit was enjoying that peak and may have thought people responded to her so readily because they appreciated who she was, but Vreni knew it was because of something she possessed that was sadly fleeting.

It was a pity they saw each other so seldom nowadays and that Vreni could not warm herself on Margrit's glow very much. The pleasure she got from the boys was not as intoxicating, and tempered a little by the fact that she was still doing their washing and cleaning. That sort of intimacy would take the shine off anyone. But her satisfaction was still wide and deep. She enjoyed their high spirits when they were getting ready to go out in the evening, and the rhythm of their strong bodies when they were working alongside her saving the hay. Their strength and bulk seemed like a kind of miracle, especially when they deferred to her or carried out a task at her instruction. It was not something she'd ever spoken about with anyone – who would care or understand? – but the sense of ownership she felt towards her children was one of her greatest life treasures. They were her fortune. She didn't need the nine francs a month per child from the canton, a fight with Peter she'd abandoned years before. She had their physical existence as her reward. There had been miscarriages along the way and one stillbirth between Ueli and Hugo which left her feeling unmoored until she had a new baby to hold. This day and every day, each of her four surviving children remained a priceless gift. They filled her up.

On the half-empty train, Vreni claimed a four-seater for herself. As soon as she had spread out her things to occupy the space, she fled straight to the toilet, returning some minutes later on a wave of relief. The countryside had retreated into the fog again, and she could not see much farther than a stone's throw from the train. Vreni closed her eyes and allowed her body to slump into the seat. She got tired so quickly these days. She did not want to be tired for the rest of her life.

It made her glad that things would be different for Margrit. When she pictured Margrit's future now, she imagined her sitting on a modern, beige-coloured sofa in one of the living rooms she had seen in the Zurich exhibition. The living room, carpeted of course, was in one of the houses where Vreni's old school friend Klara lived. She'd last visited Klara nine years before in her new home which had just been built on the outskirts of Bern. It was in a fairy-tale neighbourhood of perfectly proportioned three-bedroom houses attached in pairs, each one with a good-sized garden, and a bus at the end of the street that did a loop through the estate all day, whisking residents into the city whenever they felt the need. Vreni liked it so much she couldn't go back there. How Klara, who'd never had children, had managed to find a second tolerably handsome husband after she was widowed and had become a newly-wed again at the age of forty was difficult to fathom. But there she was, living a new life in a new place so different from their girlhood years together it might as well have been on another planet.

Never mind Klara. This was Margrit's future. She would have two children – a girl and a boy – and a husband who was an optician or a pharmacist or something in that line, a calm and quiet sort who would not mind Margrit outshining him or having a bank account or choosing their children's names or deciding what fruit trees to plant. Margrit would be friends with all the neighbours and take the bus whenever she wanted, popping her good little children over the fence into a neighbour's garden whenever she needed to dash off to get milk or more paper for her typewriter. She would be at the centre of things, the person people ran ideas past. Everyone would remark on how devoted she was to her parents; she would invite them all the time for Sunday lunch. And every year for Vreni's birthday she would take her on a boat ride on a different lake. Vreni had seen those beautiful big steamboats on Lake Zurich the summer before and once on Lake Thun when they were visiting Peter's brother. People seemed to get so excited about the mountains, but she much preferred the lakes, with the mountains in the distance. Perhaps she should mention this interest in pleasure boats to Margrit sometime, plant the seed.

Vreni was first at the door to get off in Bern, but she struggled with the opening mechanism and couldn't get it open. Flushed with irritation, she had to step back and allow a younger woman to take over. She found herself down at the far end of the train and had to walk down the long platform, being overtaken by all these faster, busier people. She was suddenly aware of her coat and shoes being shabby. Where was Margrit? On and on she walked, feeling conspicuous as a lone traveller, her suitcase catching on her leg with each step. People were gathered at the head of the train where the platform met the open concourse. She had to sidestep around other travellers embracing loved ones. Still no sign of Margrit's dear face among all these strangers. This meeting was so long arranged. They had spoken about it at home at Christmas, even looked at the timetable. Vreni had mentioned all the details again in her last letter.

The warmth of the train was draining quickly from her body as the damp winter air got in under her coat. Vreni shivered and held her collar closed with one hand. Should she wait here at the end of Platform 7 or should she walk around the station? Where was Margrit? Across the hall, the left luggage sign caught her eye. She could be one step ahead and hand her bag in now, but what if Margrit didn't see her there and they missed each other? The flow of people moved among and around each other smoothly, as if guided by the hand of an invisible weaver. It was hard to believe these crowds were here every day when she had so many days with only Peter and the boys for company now and then. An insistent thirst lodged in her throat and the suitcase was crushing her fingers. She set it down on the ground and chanted silently to herself. Don't worry, don't worry. How much of a gap was there between trams, five or ten minutes? Maybe more on Sundays. If Margrit had missed her tram she would be here in a few minutes. You're not a child, she said to herself sternly. She will come.

Vreni moved a few steps to a better position and stood with her back to the barrier at Platform 7. Travellers crossed back and forth from all directions, and after a short while the crowd thinned out, a lull between trains. One thing was clear after only a few minutes in Bern: she needed a new coat. Vreni used the time to study the coats of the women passing by. The fashion had clearly changed to something more full-skirted and she was willing to go with that. But how much did a coat cost nowadays?

At the far side next to the kiosk, some thirty metres away, a young man with his back to her was leaning against the wall with one hand. He was speaking to someone intently and, as he turned, Vreni saw the familiar plum colour of Margrit's coat. The girl pushed past him and he held out his hands after her in a dramatic gesture of entreaty, which was in no way a Swiss gesture. Margrit marched straight over to Vreni and held out her arms as she reached her mother. Before Vreni was enveloped into an embrace, she had just enough time to see that something in her daughter had changed. It was not tiredness or stress that Vreni saw, though both were in evidence in Margrit's face. It was the absence of something special. Her glow was gone.

Part II

Margrit

What a way to round off the worst week of my life. I should have just let Luigi walk by with those big loping strides of his. I should have stayed where I was, leaning against the side of the kiosk with an eye on Platform 7, but no, I had to satisfy my curiosity. Was he avoiding me or could he still help me? I had to know.

I was early for Mami, of course I was. I know how she hates being away from home – I mean everyone knows that about her. And we only have a few hours together. I didn't want to spend that time with her in a bad mood. So I made sure I got the earlier tram.

I just grabbed her before she could speak, and now I'm trying to judge from the tension in her body how cross she is. Oh God, she saw Luigi. I can't say he's a work colleague... maybe a neighbour? I'm so disappointed in him. He was upfront all along, so why did he have to get so secretive in the end? It doesn't do justice to what we had together.

I'm still holding on to Mami, and the hug is definitely going on too long. Am I going to cry? This is ridiculous. I let her go and we pull back a little and inspect each other warily. Mami's bushy hair is stuffed into a navy felt hat, which is the newest thing she has on. It might look nice with a two-piece suit or something, but it doesn't work at all with the brown overcoat and the black ankle boots. The less said about the suitcase the better. It's hard to look at her face because there's something so heartbreaking about women of that age. I don't mind really old faces, but Mami looks like a young person with a ravaged face; like she's just come through a great tragedy or something. Normally I notice it much less with her, but when I haven't seen her for a bit, it hits me how much she is wilting with age. Oh, the flowers! I left them on the ground.

'Wait here!'

I dash across to where I was standing, and there are my pink tulips. As I approach her again, I see the beginning of a smile.

'Let's start again. Welcome to Bern, Mami. It's so lovely to see you. I'm really sorry I was late. Dying to hear all your news over coffee or lunch – should we go for lunch? You must be tired. You look tired. Here, you take the flowers and let's get this case checked in over there.'

'Thanks, love. One thing at a time.'

44

The whole time I'm handing over the suitcase to left luggage, Mami is watching me the way she does, like I'm doing something exceptional, and I'm trying to think of a cover story for Luigi. Come on, what's the point in making up something silly, I'll just say he's an admirer, a no-good Italian I needed to get rid of.

Shit. How will I get through the rest of the winter without him? I met him on one of the hottest days of August. I was sunbathing in the Marzili on my own. Asking for trouble, one could say, but I had the day off and no one to go with, and I was desperate to strip off and step into the cool water. I took a bread roll and a bottle of orange and I only planned to stay for the minimum amount of time to have a swim and dry off.

Your average Swiss boy would never do what Luigi did. He just put his towel down near me – a shade too close – and started remarking on how beautiful I was. It was so ridiculous I had to laugh! I knew he didn't mean it *too* seriously and I liked that. I taught him a new word that day: rascal.

Our first two dates were in parks. We strolled in the Rose Garden and in the Kleine Schanze. I wanted to meet him at the bear pit but he said he couldn't go there – the poor bears made him cry. We strolled around and then sat down and cuddled, and he sometimes kissed me fleetingly on the neck or in the crook of my arm, as well as normal kisses. He was sweet, and the way he spoke Swiss German like a child made me smile.

On our third date we walked along the riverbank and he told me his predicament. He had a fiancée back home in Puglia, and he was saving up for her to come and live with him. She would pretend to be living with a girl and, when they both had enough money put by, they would go back home and have a big wedding. Her name was Angela and he loved her. But he wanted to keep seeing me, only if I agreed and only until Angela joined him. His reasoning was that it would be good for both of us to test a different nationality – like trying a new drink, he said. And it will stop me being lonely, he said. Then he turned his expressive brown eyes on me, showing me the potential depth of his loneliness. I burst out laughing and drew him towards me. He taught me a new word that day: *deliziosa*.

Well, seeing as I was in that special situation with Herr Fasel, and not looking for anything serious, I thought, why not? I have no time for all this fuss people make about love and heartbreak and bagging a man. I'm a modern woman, and I don't have to fit into some outdated mould. The more I thought about it, the more perfect it seemed. Luigi would not make demands of me; he would just make me thirsty and satisfy that thirst at the same time. It was about time I got more experienced anyway.

It is still a bit on the early side for lunch, but I'm not sure what to do with Mami. It's not really sight-seeing weather. Maybe the History Museum. I'm shocked when she tells me she has seven francs fifty.

'For the week?'

'For today – I'm not going to spend money in hospital, am I?'

'Well, I have about the same amount. I know a place where we can go and have a nice meal a bit later, but if you want to keep some money for magazines or chocolates or whatever, we could get a cheese tart from the bakery and go back to my room.'

She looks unsure, disappointed maybe. I need a brainwave.

'Wait, I have an idea. What about going to see a film? Hang on, I can get a paper with the cinema listings.' I'm about to fly over to the kiosk, but Mami grabs me by the sleeve.

'For heaven's sake, Margrit, will you slow down? You're as skittish as a foal. I didn't come to Bern to sit in the dark with hundreds of people. I want to see you and talk to you. So, why don't you take me to a nice café nearby and you can start by telling me about the young man you were talking to a few minutes ago.'

So then she links arms with me, which she knows I hate, and people have to dodge their way

47

around us as we walk down the Marktgasse arcades to the Capitol. The old waitress takes our order, and Mami is admiring and exclaiming at everything – the seats, the tables, the pictures on the walls. And I want to say, yes, I know, it's a café. But then the coffee cups come and they have the cream on the side in those little chocolate cups like a thimble, and that sets her off again. Until eventually she remembers what she wanted to ask.

'And, are you going to tell me about the young man who was talking to you so earnestly, the one who made you forget your mother's train?'

I don't like the way she's studying me. I take off my cardigan and drape it over the back of my chair. It's warm in here. 'That's a neighbour, Luigi.'

'Luigi?'

'Yes, Mami, he's Italian. I bumped into him at the station, he's on his way to Brig to collect his... his sister. And he was complaining about the checks they do at the border, that she might be scared by that. Or they might be delayed and miss the train back.' She nods, as if this all makes sense, so I keep going. 'And I just wanted to wish him well and move on, but then he asked me out and I said no and he started trying to persuade me. He's a talker. I got stuck with him and I didn't notice the time.'

She doesn't say anything and I realise she's playing that trick where you don't comment and just let the other person ramble on until they reveal something. So I stop and smile.

'He looked very familiar with you,' she eventually says and purses her lips into a line of disapproval.

I don't want to spend any more time on this, so I ask for a full report on each of the boys, whether they're behaving, how much work they're doing for Papi and elsewhere, how much money they're bringing in, if there's any talk of girls, and how Marcel is getting on with his studying. Mami always has lots to say about the boys, and while I keep half an ear on her answer, I'm recalling the conversation with Luigi at the station and feeling like a badly cracked vase, as if I am about to shatter all over this boring little café.

And I'm not even sure if I love Luigi properly. But I do need him and this is the worst possible time for him to drop me for Angela. This is the moment he could help by waiting for me outside work, looking the part of the devoted fiancé. If Herr Fasel could see that I had someone serious in my life, that might get me out of the situation I'm in. I guess that's part of the reason girls like to be attached, it scares off the vultures.

Mami gets up to use the ladies and I notice she's walking a bit funny. I suppose I should ask her about the health stuff, but I don't really want to hear the nitty-gritty. It's a pity I can't tell her about my problem. Or tell anyone for that matter. Luigi would have understood because he's seen another side of me and he's not judgemental. But he is on the train to Brig now and no use to me anymore.

The café is full but fairly quiet as it's mostly just men reading the papers. There is one intense game of *Jass* going on in a cloud of cigarette smoke in the corner. You don't see many women out at this time of day, at least not wives. The Sunday lunch doesn't make itself. I suppose Herr Fasel will be sitting down to a nice spread soon in his big house in Kirchenfeld. I hope he chokes.

Here she comes. She really does look tired. When she sits down, I reach over and pat her hand.

'Do you want to tell me more about the operation? Does everyone get it done at your age?'

A look of irritation crosses her face and she glances left and right as if there might be spies around us. When she speaks her voice is just above a whisper.

'I don't really want to explain here. I'll tell you more when we're somewhere more private. But the main stuff you know, I'll be in the clinic for two weeks and then one week in the convalescent home in town. And then, please God, I will be healed and back on my feet by Easter at the latest.'

'Right. And you need to be back at the station for the half-past-four bus.'

'More like four o'clock.'

'That's fine. I'll come with you on the bus to the clinic. So what's it going to be? The Alps, history or art?' She looks confused. 'I mean what museum would you like to visit?'

Mami lets out the longest sigh. 'I'm not really up to all that today – sorry, darling.'

'So what do you want to do?'

An hour later we're back at my room, and Mami has agreed to lie down. I have the blankets rolled up to make extra pillows and she looks comfortable enough. I know all about the prolapse now and I need some air. But that's fine because we've decided to have a picnic lunch in my room and I'm going off to buy lots of treats.

I'm going to the fancier bakery in Breitenrain. The walk will do me good. I'm not used to Mami being weak – it's strange. As I cross Nordring, I remember a scene from my childhood when she was in bed and too tired to move. In the memory I'm in bed with her. Why would I be in my parents' bed? There's a baby in the cradle next to the bed and he keeps crying and crying, but Mami won't move.

Those babies are no help to me now. Maybe if I had an older brother. I imagine this taller, smarter brother, someone I could confide in. He storms into the office and punches the boss in the face, knocking him out cold. There's a tiny bit of pleasure in that, just the idea of it.

How did I get it so wrong with Herr Fasel? I remember in the last few weeks of the secretarial course that Frau Wick gave this special talk to the girls. We were all horribly uncomfortable and fascinated at the same time. Luckily, she kept it short. Her advice boiled down to this: whatever you do, don't laugh when you're uncomfortable. Male colleagues will test you, they will see what they can get away with. Your laugh is the same as giving permission, so don't try and smooth things over by being nice. Be awkward and boring, and always move away from the scene when something starts.

That's all very well, but what if the laughing starts before the touching? What if you hand over too many laughs before you know what's going on? In Frau Wick's scenario, the bad guys were rude and pushy. They were not funny and charming. They did not praise you all the time and make you feel looked after, moving your desk out of the draught and buying the tea you like. They did not come into work with red eyes and look so desperately unhappy. They did not profess their profound respect for you before beginning a campaign of casual touching that seemed to reflect a special understanding between you. Here a hand on the shoulder, the upper arm, the knee, the lower back.

Enough to make you dizzy. They did not ask you to stay late and help them clear up after their birthday *apéro*. Nor were they handsome and cultured, these dangerous men. They hid their claws until it was too late.

I buy everything that catches my eye in the bakery. Bacon croissants, cheese tartlets, two slices of cream cake, a bottle of apple juice. I have some cheese and pears on the windowsill. This is going to be a feast.

I hurry back, eager to get away from the cold air and my gloomy thoughts. Frau Kaeser passes me in the hallway before I reach the stairs. She stares pointedly at my parcels and shakes her head in disapproval. She doesn't like us girls eating in our rooms, but she only gives us access to the kitchen in short time slots during the week. Does she expect us to survive on thin air?

Mami is sitting up reading one of my magazines when I come in, the one with Grace Kelly and her babies on the cover. The radio is playing folk music.

'It's cosy here.' She smiles. 'Well, what goodies have you brought back?'

'You'll see. Stay where you are while I put everything out on the tray.' I get two plates and arrange the savoury pastries with slices of pear and a spoon of Mami's own squash preserve. I take two glasses of juice and put them on the bedside table. She smooths out a patch in the middle of the bed and we sit on either side of the tray with tea towels on our laps.

'This is the life,' Mami says, tucking into her croissant.

I look around the room, the handmade rug on the floor, Frau Kaeser's bulky wardrobe and chest of drawers taking up most of the space. But the wallpaper and the curtains are fresh and bright, and the pictures I bought myself of Paris, New York and the South of France are pleasing to the eye. All clean and tidy, the way I like things, the way Mami taught me. It strikes me that this is the room of a younger woman, someone who has not yet had to compromise on who she believes herself to be. There is no sign of the turbulence of the past half a year.

When we have eaten our fill, I tidy away the left-overs for later, and we have a brief disagreement about how the cost of the meal should be divided. I let Mami win. The music has switched to old-style orchestral dance pieces.

I sit on a cushion on the floor, my back against the wardrobe, and try to draw Mami out. The more she talks, the better. She tells me that she decided to stand up to Papi about the sandwiches for the vote, and how she relented in the end. We both laugh at the picture of Papi making atrocious sandwiches. I ask her what her instructions were for my young cousin. That girl has her work cut out. And then I remember the new foster boy.

When I was home for Christmas, Ruedi was still terribly shy and only spoke when spoken to. The poor mite, he didn't know whether to sit or stand when the family was around. He made the rest of us feel awkward. Mami tried to keep him occupied, but the weather was terrible and there was only so much that needed doing. One afternoon, I dug out our old games from the cupboard in the hallway and taught him how to play Ludo and Jass. We became a regular duo and I discovered that he could smile. He told me he wanted to work on the trains when he grew up. He'd been on a train once. The ticket inspector made a big impression. I started calling him *Kontrolleur* during our games and he loved that.

'How's Ruedi getting on?'

'The Home child?'

'Yes, Ruedi. I thought he was so sweet when I saw him at Christmas. So willing to help.'

'He broke the milk jug yesterday. Just dropped it straight on the floor when Hugo came into the kitchen and startled him.'

'Oh dear, but how is he getting on? Does he still tremble when the room gets crowded?'

'He's fine. You were too familiar with him, Margrit. It's not a good idea to show affection to these children. They get the wrong idea.'

'A bit of kindness, surely?'

'Kindness is one thing, I have never been unkind. But a certain distance is easier for them to deal with. Do you think the nuns go around hugging and kissing them?'

'They have a hard life.' I feel pressure on my throat like a dam.

'Exactly.'

'With no one to protect them.'

'I do protect them. I protect Ruedi. In our house he is kept warm, well dressed and well fed. He goes to school and Papi helps him with his sums. None of us has ever raised a hand to him.' Two spots of red, each the size of a five-franc coin, appear on her cheeks and she swings her legs back onto the floor. 'You know what the most important thing is for boys like that at the bottom of the pile? They have to learn how to work, how to be useful. He'll be out on his own in a few years, you know. They don't stay cute for long.'

My breath becomes agitated. 'I think if someone comes under your protection, you should show more than kindness. Why not a little love?' And that's when, with horror, I realise that I am about to be engulfed with tears.

'Love? Spoken like a girl who has never worked a day in service in her life. Did they love you in commercial college? Do they love you in the surveyor's office?'

I cover my face with my hands and try to stifle a sudden burst of sobs. It is no use. I am overcome. Mami's arms are around my shoulders almost instantly. She kneels beside me and tries to soothe me with her voice, repeating her old name for me, *little treasure*. I can't remove my hands from my face. I am so ashamed of my weakness and my foolishness. But she stays there and waits until the sobs gradually subside and I am just weeping silently, leaning against her comforting solid form.

After a time, she leads me to the bed and fetches a wet facecloth to pat my face. I avoid her eye, but she is not going anywhere. She sits and holds my hand.

'Something is lying on your heart like a stone, my girl. Do you want to talk about it now, or would you like me to make tea first? Because we are going to talk about it. You'd better accept that.'

I manage to croak the word 'tea' and she sets off for the kitchen with my teapot and a cupful of dried chamomile flowers. What have I done? Giving in to tears is not my style. Crying in front of another person is practically against my religion. And now suddenly she's the expert on me? She has no idea what my life is like. What does she know about the world, a woman who is afraid to go to the village in case she meets some other housewife? It's ridiculous. And why is she not a bit softer with Ruedi? What about that word 'motherly'?

A spasm of guilt hits me and I cover my face again. My mother loves me. She has done nothing wrong and she is on my side. The person I should be angry with is the man who is even older than her, a so-called man of the world who uses his position to dominate other people. It's not just me, it's how he treats the younger surveyors and the apprentice. God knows how he treats his wife. I don't want to think about her. I turn to face the wall and stare at the blankness of my misery. So this is what it is to lose hope. It's like being in a deep, dark forest with no paths and no light coming through the canopy of trees; nothing like my forest at home which is bright and welcoming in every season. This is the thorny, overgrown forest from the most frightening fairy tales, the worst place you'd want to be caught wandering, lost and helpless.

Mami returns and we drink our tea together. She stays quiet and watchful while the last, shuddering sighs leave my body. Finally, she takes the empty cup from me and sets it down on the bedside table. She puts her hand on mine and waits.

'You're supposed to be the patient,' I say, and we share a melancholy smile.

'Is it the Italian man?' she asks.

I snatch my hand away, annoyed again. If she's going to think in these silly old black-and-white terms, how can I explain anything to her?

'No,' I can hear my tone of voice, like a petulant teenager. 'No,' softer this time. 'Luigi is more like a friend, Mami. I mean it. He is a decent young man. We were seeing each other for a while and this week it came to an end. That's all.'

'So he didn't break your heart?'

'No, to be fair, no. But I must have cared for him more than I realised. I will miss him.'

'But you're not... in trouble, are you?' Before I can object, she is promising to love any child of mine like her own.

'No, Mami, it's not that. I'm not pregnant. I'm in a different situation, a bad situation. I don't know how to describe it. If I was a character in one of your detective books, I would say I'm being blackmailed.'

Her face strips back from shock to sympathy to anger.

'I can only tell you if you promise to stay calm. Please?'

I can see her pulling hard on the reins of those runaway feelings. She doesn't want to scare me. Eventually, she clasps her hands together as if in prayer and nods to me.

'I'm ready,' she says.

This is it, I guess. I ask her to stand, and from under my mattress I pull out four envelopes and hand them to her.

'Herr Fasel gave me these.'

She counts the money and looks at me in consternation. 'Three hundred francs! What the devil is going on?'

'It's complicated.'

'I'm trying to be patient here, Margrit. Tell me, what is this money for?'

I can't look at her. 'He was expecting something in return. He called it a bonus, for my good work, but it was more like a down payment. I tried to refuse the money, but he wouldn't take it back. And so I took it and I thought, well, he can't force me. He'll get the message eventually and give up.'

'But he didn't give up?'

'No.' An unwelcome image of Herr Fasel on Friday evening intrudes into my mind. His face, close to mine. I can see the broken blood vessels on his cheeks, the pinpricks of stubble and the deep grooves on either side of his mouth as he leans in to kiss me.

'But you said you were being blackmailed? I don't understand.'

I fear she won't understand even when I try to explain. I hope I can find the right words. 'Everything changed on Friday. It was his birthday and he brought two bottles of white wine into work plus six glasses. All nicely packed in a special basket. He said we could all finish early, and he called me into his office to help him set up the *apéro*. As we were putting out the tablecloth and the glasses, he held me by the hips when he needed to move around me, stood a bit too close, that kind of thing. It wasn't anything out of the ordinary. I just let it go.

'Then everyone came in and stood around for a while with their glasses of wine, and Herr Fasel refilled my glass once or twice. After the first toast and the birthday wishes, the conversation was stilted. Nobody wanted to mention politics, so they talked about ice hockey and their deadlines and I listened and smiled. I was thinking about Luigi, who's been avoiding me this week, and figuring out what I would say to him. I was distracted. I had no idea what this was leading up to.

'Of course, the lads were all anxious to get going and start their weekend. One minute I was in the group, letting the conversation wash over me, the next minute they were all putting on their coats and scarpering out the door. He asked me to wash the glasses for him while he tidied up.'

I am shaking, but I want to get this story clear in my mind, too. Mami nods at me to carry on, her face grave. 'I thought he was just flirting with me and that I could manage it. I never dreamed he would dare to force himself on me. When I came back from the kitchen with the glasses on a tray, he pointed at his desk and I put them down there. Next thing I knew, his hands were all over me. I staggered backwards and he pinned me against the wall and was trying to undress us both. My skirt was up around my waist and the whole scene felt so unreal, as if this outrageous thing was happening to someone else. That was probably the alcohol. Mami, I nearly let it happen. It seemed inevitable, out of my hands. I'm not a passive person, and I can't understand why I almost submitted to him. He was so determined, so full of certainty.'

'Oh Margrit, no.' She covers her mouth and I look away again. I have to keep going.

'Over his shoulder I saw his coat and hat on the stand. And I thought, this is my boss. This is not acceptable. I was suddenly more furious than afraid, and with that anger I pushed him off and shouted, "No!" We stood there facing each other, clothes in disarray, both of us panting like wrestlers. A sly look came over his face, and he took a step closer.

'He started telling me I would never get a book-keeping job or any job, not when everyone in Bern heard about me thieving from his company. Then he named the amounts he had given me each month – October, November, December, January. He knew it all off by heart. He said he could prove I had taken the money from his desk. He called me a tramp and worse names, all the time coming closer. He said I knew exactly what I was doing from the day I walked into the office. Then when he was right up close, he said: "One of two things is going to happen here. Either you will submit to me or I will ruin you." And then he kissed me, and that was the most horrible thing of all.' A shiver runs through my body at the memory and Mami keeps her hand firm on my knee.

'Take your time,' she says, her voice clotted with emotion. I take a deep breath and continue.

'I wriggled out of his grip and told him to stop. While I was grabbing my things and trying to get out of there as quick as I could, he followed me about, talking and talking, repeating his threat and telling me how important he was in Bern and that we would continue this discussion after work on Monday. I remember his exact parting words. He gripped my arm hard and said, "You have started something with me, girl, and you will see it through."'

All the time I'm speaking, I have my eyes cast down, focusing on the floor. Finally, I turn and look into Mami's eyes. Impossible as it seems, she radiates sympathy and rage at the same time. She kneads her face with one big strong hand and I reach out to still the movement.

'That man,' she says. 'That man will pay.'

There is so much venom in her words, it warms me. She hates him too. She is on my side. But there's nothing we can do. I try to tell her.

'He's a member of the *Bürgergemeinde* – he knows the whole city government, works on all the municipal projects. Nothing happened, I mean he didn't actually hurt me and even if he did, I can't prove anything. Who would believe me anyway?' I grab the envelopes from the floor and hold them up like pieces of evidence. But evidence of what?

Mami shook her head slowly. 'Yes, he's a so-called respectable man. But that's his weak point, too. He's married, isn't he? And he lives here in Bern. What time is it?'

'What? No! You're not doing anything. We can't do anything.'

'You may be afraid of him, love, but I'm not.' She holds my wrist and looks at the time. 'It's only two o'clock. Plenty of time.'

'Mami, we can't go to his house!'

'Why not? What was your plan?'

She's got me there. 'I don't know. I was going to skip work tomorrow. Maybe never go back.'

'And then what? Let him spread stories about you and ruin your chance to get another job? Go back to the village? No.'

'I don't want you to say anything to Papi or the boys.' Alarm fills my chest like rushing water.

'Of course not. Listen, we have to deal with the here and now. Do you have a key to the office?'

All signs of Mami's tiredness are gone. She is all business now, issuing instructions. The more I listen to her, the more I can see the merit in her plan. I didn't think she could be so strong-minded. I put myself in her hands. On our way to the office, she leans on me a little and I grip her arm tighter, glad to take some weight.

'I have something to ask. This run-in with Herr Fasel, is that the worst thing that's ever happened to you with a man?'

'Yes.'

'Good,' she almost smiles. 'You'll be all right, don't worry.'

In the office, there is no sign of Friday's drama. I take my typewriter and some headed paper and sit at one of the window desks where the light is better. I compose a glowing reference and throw in words he likes to use, like 'reliable', 'efficient' and 'flexible'. I pull the page from the roller and hand it to Mami.

'Do you really think this will work?'

She scans the page quickly and nods.

'Nice,' she says. 'Type it up two more times. Where do you keep the envelopes?'

We leave everything as it was and I have one last look around from the doorway. Mami puts her hand on my shoulder. I was so excited starting here last spring. After working in Loeb for two years, this was a real step up. Not selling stockings and perfume anymore but calculating the costs on huge building projects. I loved everything about it at first – getting dressed up for the day, talking about steel girders and concrete, taking coffee breaks with the men and handling files. The junior surveyors relied on me much more than the last assistant, they said. I practically trained in the new lad.

'And now for part two,' she says.

It's after three now. We have to criss-cross Bern to get to the hospital by five. I hope I'm not making a massive mistake.

The conductor sees us trying to hurry and leans out to keep the tram door open. Mami is out of puff, so I thank him kindly for both of us and pay the fare. We have to change at Casino and take the tram that crosses the Kirchenfeld bridge. Here we lose ten anxious minutes. Mami looks paler than before and her jaw is clenched. Perhaps I should try and change her mind, cancel this whole adventure. She may not be the best judge of what to do, someone who has spent most of her life between the yard and the kitchen. But she is right about one thing – my plan was pathetic.

The one thing we disagree about is the money. I want to throw it back in his face, but she thinks I should keep it, consider it my property now. Besides,

I'll need something to live on until I get a new job, she reminds me. When I mention my savings account, she is horrified. That money is not to be touched. What, not ever? I ask. Apparently savings are not there to use in times of need, they should only be used for something substantial that you will always have. Like a husband, I joke.

There's little room for being light-hearted now. We climb aboard the next tram and sit together. Mami sighs and leans her head on her hand.

'It's only two stops,' I remind her. After that I'm not exactly sure where the street is, but I have the address. We will have to ask someone for Motta Street. The tram shudders and jingles, and our stop is announced.

The houses on the street are beautiful. They must be from the last century, graceful townhouses three and four storeys high, painted different colours. It looks like a different country. Very different from the plain apartment buildings and run-down houses in my part of town.

My stomach is swirling with pure dread. I think I might be sick. We are four houses away, three, two. I pull Mami back.

'What if he's not at home?'

'Come, now,' she says gently. 'I will do the talking.'

'And if he closes the door in our face?'

'We won't give him a chance.'

'He might call the police.' I know I sound like a baby, but I can't go through with this. I want to stop, turn back. We shouldn't be here, disturbing this man on his Sunday at home. I can't put another foot forward. Stupid tears spring from my eyes. My breath becomes jagged. Mami tuts in exasperation. She turns and faces me, reaching up to put her hands on my shoulders.

'Look at me. We have come all the way here and our business won't take long. In five minutes, this will be done, and you will be rid of him for good. So, pull yourself together and let me do this for you. I'm not afraid. Agreed, Margrit?'

The house is just metres away. He might be playing a board game with his children or reading a magazine by the fire or whatever those kinds of fathers do on a Sunday. It is now or never. Mami's hands suddenly grip my shoulders more sharply. She is looking past me. 'Is this him?' she whispers, and I turn to see a figure approaching with a familiar confident gait. Herr Fasel, on home ground.

What happens next is almost comical. Nobody knows how to react, least of all Herr Fasel, who can't tell if this is an ambush or a strange coincidence. I end up introducing my mother to my boss as if this is a normal chance meeting, and they shake hands.

She has to take the lead. I think, please let her take the lead and get us out of here.

'Margrit was just about to show me your lovely home,' Mami says, a dangerous edge to her voice that he probably cannot interpret. 'When were these houses built?'

'The street was built in phases. This row is from the 1890s,' he answers, frowning in bewilderment.

'Well, we didn't come here to talk about local history,' she says and takes the envelope from me. 'In fact, it's just as well we ran into you outside, so we don't have to disturb your family.' I notice she is refining her dialect to mimic his.

'Disturb my family? What do you mean?' he says. But not like an innocent man – the colour in his cheeks gives him away. I am immune from him with my mother standing here. It's a good feeling.

'Family is important, I agree. We were so pleased when Margrit got the job in your office. We brought her up to work hard and we expected that she would be treated well. It's not too much to ask, surely, that a girl should be treated well?'

'I'm not discussing employment matters in the street. If you'll excuse me.' He makes to move past us, but Mami blocks the path and raises her voice ever so slightly.

'Oh, I feel it's much better to talk here, out in the open, though I'm sure your home is lovely.

This won't take long. You see, Margrit tells me everything. Everything. And as far as I'm concerned, she cannot work for you anymore. Not another day. I won't allow it.'

'You won't allow it?' He looks her up and down. Though he tries to muster an expression of contempt, the nervousness is plain to see in his eyes.

'We're the same generation, Herr Fasel. Let's deal with this in a reasonable way. Now, I have three copies of a reference letter for Margrit here for you to sign. Give him the keys, Margrit. You won't be seeing my daughter again. But if a future employer asks, you will speak highly of her. The extra money you gave her, the money she neither asked for nor wanted, she will keep to cover the time it takes her to find a new job. It seems to me that's the best way to put all this behind us.'

'I don't know who you think you are.'

'I am this girl's mother, and you can be glad you are dealing with me and not her father. You can also be glad I am dealing with you and not your wife. So, do you have a pen?'

He shoots me a look of pure spite and pulls a pen out of his inside pocket. Leaning the letters on Mami's proffered handbag, he signs three times and then walks around us as if we were vagrants, and hurries into his house.

I throw my arms around Mami and squeeze her lovely wide body tight. It's our second hug today, but this one is all for her. We turn back towards the tram stop. I could run with joy and relief, but I keep a slow pace with her.

'I can't believe you did that. You were amazing. *Do you have a pen?* My God, the way you spoke to him. Like a judge or something.' I'm giggling.

'He didn't like it, that's for sure.'

'He didn't like it one bit!' I could sing out loud. But why is she so calm? 'Mami, you did so well. Aren't you pleased?'

She smiles weakly. 'I just hope we've heard the last of him, the swine. That took more effort than I expected. I feel like I've been in a real fight. Look, my hands are shaking.'

New thoughts are crowding into my head. Where will I work next? Will I be able to earn as much and keep my cosy room? Maybe people will be suspicious that I left this job so soon. How will I explain that? What if I meet my workmates in town? What will I say to them?

Mami is speaking, but I have to ask her to repeat herself.

'Do we have enough time to collect the suitcase and get to the hospital by five?'

'We have plenty of time,' I assure her, but everything is taking so long. We see a tram arrive but miss it because we can't get across the road quickly enough. I have exhausted her with all this walking. At least there are benches at the tram stop. Mami gets her breath back and starts talking about boats and lakes and, honestly, I can hardly believe in the summer right now. Bern has never looked so grey and dreary, every patch of grass on this avenue worn down to mud with a few thinning streaks of dirty green. Will anything ever bloom again?

I can't wait to tell Luigi about the confrontation with Herr Fasel – and then it hits me. I can't tell Luigi about this. Luigi has cut me off. We've been seeing each other every second or third day. I haven't seen my friends from Loeb for months.

Luigi and I have our favourite doorways and cinema seats and cafés. We know every inch of the Old Town – the bric-a-brac shops, the cellar dance clubs, the best pizza restaurant owned by the sad Sardinian with the big moustache. It doesn't seem possible that he will take Angela to all those places. Maybe he will look for new favourite places with her. I would prefer that.

Near the train station, I deposit Mami at the right bus stop and scoot off to get her suitcase. She is definitely wincing a lot more now and I notice tiny beads of sweat on her upper lip. The sooner she is safely in her hospital room, the better. I won't let her do a single thing after the operation. I will visit every day.

Yet another journey on public transport. We are squeezed in together on a narrow double seat and the bus driver grinds through the gears as he climbs the hill to the hospital. We've been on the move for hours and I picture us like two little figures on a board game moving around the squares of the city.

'Are you OK, Mami?' She has her eyes closed.

'I'm fine. Just a bit cold and tired. Nearly there.'

'And you won't tell Papi about today?'

'No, it won't help anyone. You just do your best to get a new job quickly and we'll say nothing until it's sorted. You have good qualifications. It will be fine.'

As we wait at a junction, I notice a 'yes' poster I haven't seen before. It shows a smiling man casting his 'yes' vote. He has a lipstick kiss on his cheek. One way of getting their attention, I suppose. I'm not one for politics, but this vote feels like an important test. Either we are in this together, men and women, or we are not.

For the first time ever, I wonder how long I can do this. There are jobs in Bern, but the pay is so low. Maybe it would be different if I had a nice little apartment with my own bath and kitchen. How long can you live alone in one room? It seems like the solution for a better life is to find a man. I don't think I'm against marriage, I just don't know if the right kind of man exists for me. Someone who wouldn't take over my life. Luigi was like that, but I was only a temporary distraction for him.

'The hospital, they just announced the hospital,' Mami gives me a dig in the ribs, and I press the stop button just in case.

The building is very grand and it looks nice with so many windows lit up. We follow the signs to admissions and come to a reception area with about a dozen women waiting, some with companions. We have to step over various bags and suitcases to get to an empty seat. I take Mami's letter and stand a polite distance behind the person being served at the admissions desk. Everyone's eyes are on me. Tough. There's no obvious queueing system so, until it's clear, I'm standing here.

I focus on the woman behind the glass so I can get her attention when the time comes. She looks much too old and too rich to be working here, or anywhere for that matter. She's wearing a classically cut pale blue tweed jacket over a cream silk blouse. From what I can see, her brooch seems to be in the shape of a frog. What an odd thing to wear. Her dyed hair, several shades too dark for her colouring, sits in tight waves from the parting down, like corrugated iron. The whole effect, combined with heavy red lipstick and bejewelled glasses, is jarring. If she was twenty-five and in Paris it would be fine, but this is Bern and she must be over sixty.

She interrupts her exchange to speak to me, raising her voice just enough. 'I'm calling out names as we go. You may take a seat.'

Is there anything duller than having to wait in a medical place? Doctor, dentist, you name it, time seems to crawl along. They have the most boring reading material in the world, or, in this case, nothing. I fetch Mami a glass of water and we watch the crowd thin out. It's not yet five and they have to get through the four-thirty people first. A cleaner in a blue housecoat comes to empty the bin.

Finally, when everyone else has been seen to, we get our moment with Miss Sparkly Glasses. It turns out she's kind, smiling at Mami to reassure her that she is in safe hands here. She takes all of Mami's details patiently and starts filling in a card for her to take with her to the ward. And then I get a strange feeling. Every time I turn around the cleaner is staring at us. She is pretending to straighten chairs, but I can tell she is moving closer and she's listening. My reference letters! I left the envelope on my seat. As I pass the woman on my way to collect the envelope, I give her a dirty look, but she looks back at me without a hint of shame. I can't help it: I measure her looks against mine and it bothers me that she is possibly, by some standards, better-looking. Even though she is older and not wearing any make-up, with her ash blonde hair pulled back in a hairband like a schoolgirl.

Mami is on her feet and I practically drag her to the lift. I've had enough of this hospital, the smell, the bland decor, the depressed women. We get up to the ward and find her bed, in a room with three others. I don't want to be introduced so I leave her case on the bed and call her out to the hallway again.

She wants to start a chat with me, but we've been through everything. I humour her for a little while and then I say it's getting dark, I should go. The cleaner appears from around the corner and stops when she sees us. She turns and goes back the way she came.

'There she is again. She was staring at us downstairs.'

But Mami is not listening. She wants to tell me the time of the operation, again. I guess she needs reassurance.

'I know, I know, you said. Look, I'm going to come to the desk at lunchtime tomorrow and ask how you are and when I can see you. Now I'll be free at visiting hours and I'll see you every day if you like. And I'll bring you whatever you need.'

We embrace and I try to squeeze some of that tension out of her.

'What a day,' she says.

'Yes, what a day. Thanks for saving me. You know you saved me today. It will be a new start for both of us tomorrow.'

'And everything will be fine.'

'Everything will be better than before.'

As I turn the corner towards the stairwell, I see the cleaner halfway up the stairs to the next floor. She is holding the banister and facing away from me. I stop at the foot of the stairs, daring her to look around. She scurries away.

Part III

Esther

When I heard the name Sutter, I almost yelped with shock. It was all I could do to straighten up and stand quietly with the commotion going on in my head. This was her, this lump of a farmer's wife with her hat sitting crooked on her head. I had written that name and address so carefully in my best handwriting, not once or twice but five times. Five envelopes, five stamps. As a mother, I had hoped she would understand and show some mercy. Instead I was ignored. Those months of waiting ignited all the old feelings of worthlessness but also the old anger.

The daughter, what a haughty look she gave me, caught me staring and I could see she felt something was wrong. Yes, I could have told her, something is very wrong. And your mother has played her part.

I needed to check that I had heard the ward number correctly. I went up to the second floor, and there they were in the corridor, standing so close, as if they were trying to pass something secret to each other before they parted. Invisible gifts between mother and daughter.

You see a lot of things when you work in a hospital. You see how the well are in a hurry to get away from the sick, how deeply they breathe in the outside air when they get to the open door, how poorly they disguise their relief. That girl couldn't wait to say her goodbyes.

I'm supposed to work until six, but I return to my room in a daze. So much thinking to do. I wrap myself in the blanket from the bed and sit sideways across the windowsill, hugging my knees to my chest. I don't have much there to show for my years on this earth; no jewellery or furniture of my own, just a few clothes and photographs. If I was allowed to put something on the wall, I might be able to make it look more cheerful. My coat on the back of the door is the only personal touch. But I am glad to have a safe place, thanks to Fräulein Vogelsang who understands my predicament and actually wants to help. I wonder if she also recognised the name and address when she checked Frau Sutter in earlier. She was the one who found the contact details for me last September.

Frau Verena Sutter, Obere Matte, Mendenswil. Those few words contain all my hopes and a lifetime of despair.

I was seven years old when I was taken. I'm grateful that I was not younger, as I met other children along the way who were Yenish like me but didn't realise that about themselves. They did not know what it meant when the teachers and other kids made comments, but I knew. It meant us and them. It meant there was another way to live and speak and be.

My family was wary of school. But once you were registered in a commune, they made it very hard to say no. We spent the cold months in the same village near Solothurn a few years in a row. The other kids walked home alone, but our mothers waited outside school every day before the bell rang. They were taking precautions. The day the people came for me, though, it was during the morning break and no one was around to shout stop.

This is when I learned it is a bad idea to ask the authorities for help. You might get some money, but then the snooping starts, and the disapproval and people acting like they don't like the smell of you.

My abiding memory of my parents from that last winter is of my mother dressing my father's leg in the evenings. He had suffered a gash in his calf months before on a building job, but the wound kept weeping no matter how many times she cleaned it. He sat in a bentwood chair by the stove, and cursed quietly while she tended to him. The others were asleep next to me, but I liked to stay awake for this scene because she was so tender to him then. I waited for the moment when she finished and stood to kiss him on the forehead. He rested his big hand on her hip and I could see her smile mirror his. It pleased me to think that she loved him, too, the same way she loved us. The rest of the time they were more like fellow workers, too busy striving against the world to stop and look at each other.

Somebody somewhere decided that our little home was too full and too free. They took three of us away and left the younger ones. They wanted to see children in straight lines with clean dresses and plaited hair. They wanted us meek.

I put in my years in the Home. I had my own magic trick of turning myself into a tree at will. If there was a beating to be taken, I took it on my wooden flank. If there was name-calling, it did not penetrate the grain. I made alliances with the strong kids and the wild ones, and I stole what I needed whenever I got the chance. But I wasn't a typical troublemaker. I took care with my schoolwork and did my chores without being asked twice. I don't think they knew what to make of me.

It wasn't the worst apprenticeship for life. I learned to survive without love, how to make myself useful and how to endure hardship. I knew what boys wanted from girls and quickly realised men were just the same. I could kick and scratch and bite if needed.

By fifteen, I was really too old for the Home but was considered a great help so the director was slow to find a placement for me. The war was still on and people were tired of the strain of it all. They were a bit less concerned about having a girl of the roads under their roof. Eventually, I was sent to live with a family who ran a gardening and tree nursery business. They lived in a big, old house with lots of windows, pretty as a postcard.

I was supposed to be looking after the younger kids in the family, but what I really loved was tending to the rows and rows of plants outdoors. Every chance I got I was out there, offering to water the tomato plants, the baby spinach and lettuces and all the berry bushes so they would look their finest when people came to buy.

Because all the private gardens were meant to be used for vegetables, the business had to concentrate on selling the useful stuff like seeds, seedlings and saplings – but people still craved a splash of colour. For those who still wanted to be house-proud, the business stocked a few flowers for window boxes. I had never seen such intense colours. The pinks and reds were my favourite.

I considered myself lucky not to be sent to a farm or to an old lady like my two closest friends had been. There were people coming and going here and interesting things to see. The work was light, and the children weren't much trouble. I was familiar with minding younger children and these were happier and healthier than the children I was used to dealing with. I congratulated myself for landing on my feet.

I had thoughts of going to look for my family, but I didn't know where to start. They had been scattered to the four winds and it seemed wise to stay put in this place, at least until the war was over and we could cross borders again. We used to spend time in France in the old days, but the authorities had become so strict about papers that my people were lying low.

And then Christoph Lappert came along, freshly released from military service. He was soon to be twenty-one, as he told everyone who would listen, and very pleased about it. Placed under guardianship when his father died four years earlier, he was looking forward to finally being free to choose where he could work and live. His mother had problems with her nerves and had gone to live with a sister, I later learned. Christoph never talked about her. The guardian had chosen a gardener's apprenticeship for him and sent him to our place to finish the final year, interrupted by his two years in the military.

As soon as he was twenty-one, Christoph planned to move to Zurich and get work in one of the top hotels. His father had worked in a famous hotel on Lake Brienz and filled Christoph's head with stories of glitz and glamour. I think Christoph hoped he could learn how to be rich from observing rich people. It seemed as good a plan as any.

The house was on the outskirts of the village, surrounded by rows of young trees waiting for a home. Some were waist-high and some taller than me before they were dug up and transplanted. I liked to walk out there at dusk when the children were getting their bedtime hugs and kisses. Christoph was renting a room in a restaurant and had found a way to pilfer schnapps. I was surprised the first time I came across him among the trees, his eyes glinting in the dusk. We already had an easy way with each other from crossing paths at work.

Christoph was not interested in me – why should he have been? I mean, he liked to be with me, but more as if I were a pet than a person. He liked to tell stories about his active service. He had witnessed some accidents, all the crazy excavating they were doing in the Alps, blasting indoor caverns to hide all the men and equipment. I heard a lot of detail about broken bones and legs being crushed. He talked about the time he spent at the border, turning away refugees and interning deserters, patrolling for smugglers at night. It sounded exciting. He had learned how to drive and his first purchase when he had control of his own money was going to be a motorbike. He was very sour about the guardian managing his affairs and doling out a tiny allowance. I had never met my guardian properly, although I remembered his visits to the Home when I would be given some cleaning to do so that I could be pointed out to him looking industrious. When Christoph got tired of talking about himself, we cuddled and he told me I was the best-looking girl with the best body he'd ever had the pleasure to touch. I lived for those minutes. But I was careful not to drink and not to go too far with him because I didn't want to get kicked out by the family.

I became an expert in Christoph's plans and opinions. I suppose it suited him that I was more of a quiet person who kept her thoughts and her history to herself. He probably saw me as something blank and neutral, like soil, and he wanted to fill me with his own colours. Because I was unaccustomed to attention, I blossomed in the light he shone on me.

It turned out our birthdays were a week apart. I would turn sixteen just before he became an adult. Christoph read great significance into this coincidence and gradually started weaving me into his plans. He was ready to move on, but reluctant to leave me behind. The fact that he was so attached to me transformed my days. I was happy for the first time in years. I sang as I worked and joined in the fun when the children were high-spirited. We began to be a little more open in front of the others, exchanging a kiss in greeting, no longer hiding our smiles. If only that summer could have been preserved in a jar like the fruit that stored up its sweetness all around us.

Christoph went ahead to Zurich with a good letter of recommendation and an apprenticeship under his belt. He was going to send for me as soon as he was on his feet. If the only way we could be together was for us to get married, so be it, he said. The mistress didn't object to this talk of marriage, she had married young herself. But there would be some legal hoops to jump through, she said.

The war dragged on and there were no rich people coming to Christoph's hotel, at least not the sort he had imagined. Just boring businessmen from Germany and different parts of Switzerland. People who had not come there to have a good time. He was nowhere near his goal of buying a motorbike. A colleague told him he should go to Montreux, where an assortment of high-society types and rich refugees were sitting out the war. There he would find gambling and jazz and champagne – much better tips, too.

So he changed locations and soon his letters were coming from the other direction, and we were counting down the days to being together again. My mind was so taken up with Christoph, I did not trouble myself to open up to the people I lived with. Perhaps I did not know how. I regret that now because they were good people who wished the best for me. And they could have helped me later when I needed friends and believed I had none.

Arrangements were made between him, my guardian and my host family, and we got married shortly after my seventeenth birthday. We had all decided he was trustworthy. He was definitely hard-working and he had waited so patiently. All the signs were good, and I began my new life as Frau Lappert.

Christoph was lonely in Montreux. People made fun of his accent and he was stuck doing outside work and maintenance instead of serving people. Needless to say, no rich person gave him a second glance. At first, he was delighted to have me there. We had both anticipated this so much. I didn't enjoy the physical side as much as he did, but I was proud to be a married woman, and things were more comfortable when I started as a chambermaid and we put our money together.

Looking back, it seems as if all the ingredients were there for us to do well as a couple. We celebrated the end of the war together and he started being given more responsibility, collecting guests from the train station and so on. Christoph opened an account and we put our savings in there.

I never tired of the view of the lake, especially on cloudy and stormy days when all the drama of nature played out against the backdrop of the Swiss and French Alps. I must have remembered some French from my childhood travels because I picked up the basics quickly and my accent was much better than Christoph's. He was none too pleased about that so I tried to speak as little as possible in front of him.

There were some problems between us and they were caused by his moods. Christoph became more and more dissatisfied with his lot, and he complained to me about all sorts of things – money was a favourite topic, or it could be the way someone had spoken to him at work or something demeaning he was asked to do. There were also the times he thought I wasn't enthusiastic enough in bed. On evenings when these bitter complaints started, I tried to be interested and to agree with him, but he was not content with that. He twisted my words or found a lack of sympathy in my behaviour. Even when I stopped cooking or whatever I was doing, it was not enough to appease him and, on the worst days, he came close to hitting me. He would pound the furniture or the wall instead. The anger in the room snatched the breath from my lungs.

It was not the first time I had seen men with this weakness. It seemed like the way of things, and I tried to content myself with the good times and to look for ways to improve his mood. A lot of the time I succeeded and I think I would have been able to continue like that for years, but he wasn't.

Christoph was cruel in one particular way that I found unforgivable. He would not help me find my family. He would not let me go looking on my own and refused to give me any practical help. He never explained why, but I think he did not like the thought of being connected to people even lower than him in society. He often complained of not having any capital and I could tell that he thought marrying me had been a financial mistake for him. I asked for very little and tried to contribute as much as possible of my wages to our savings.

We were three years together when Ruedi was born, at the height of the cherry blossom. Christoph was proud and pleased for a while. Ruedi's christening was probably the best day we had. The weather was glorious, all the flowers on the lakefront in bloom, pretty as a picture against the sparkling water. Christoph was proud because his older brother Alfred came with his wife. They had no children and I could see that Christoph felt like the bigger man for a change. His brother was much more successful than him, running a garage back in Sion. By asking them to be godparents, Christoph had forced them to come.

I was proud, too. I'd always been so skinny, but my shape had changed since the pregnancy and I loved that. Here I was, a mother, a heavier, rounder me, living in the most beautiful place in the country with a healthy baby who had just discovered his smile.

But when the novelty wore off, it was clear that Christoph didn't like the disruption of the baby in the house and the fact that I wasn't bringing in money anymore. I could not manage his moods so well now that we were three. I was too tired and there was much more to do. Things got worse.

One day, when Ruedi was around five months old, I was doing some washing at the sink. He was at such a lovely stage. I'd made a little nest for him in the playpen and he was entertaining himself in there with his favourite odds and ends from the kitchen. He was happy as long as he knew I was nearby. I was singing an old song, one of the scraps of songs and rhymes from my early years that had come back to me since he was born.

Christoph walked in and caught me around the waist. I froze with my hands in the water, afraid to make a false move. But he just kissed me and let go.

'What's that you're singing? Is it foreign?'

'I don't know, just an old children's song. It's not foreign, it's...' I didn't want to mention that this was a song from my family. He didn't like being reminded about my background. But I needn't have worried. Christoph had other things on his mind.

He sat at the table and started to eat an apple. 'I met a guy from Sion today. He knows Alfred. This guy is just back from London. *London*, would you believe? Can you stop that for a minute, Esther? I'm talking.'

I quickly rinsed and dried my hands and sat down to give him my full attention.

'Do you know that the most expensive hotel in London was founded by a Valais man? César Ritz came from Sion, or went to school there. That's right. The Swiss have a great reputation in London. There's a big rush going on there with hotels reopening and refurbishing after the war. Customers want to enjoy the good things in life again.'

'The way people like to eat and drink their fill after a funeral.'

'What? You say the oddest things. Anyway, this guy is going back soon. He just came to Switzerland on a short visit because his mother's sick.'

Ruedi had been patient so far, even though Christoph hadn't greeted him. He had followed the chat with a wooden spoon in his mouth, dribbling into his cotton neck scarf. But he picked up a tin cup and began to bash the side of his makeshift prison. It was so sweet. He wanted to join in.

'Jesus, can you make him stop that noise?'

For the next two weeks, all he talked about was London. It was the same excitement I'd seen when I first met him. He had borrowed an English hotel guide from work and studied it like it was an almanac of the future, which, in a sense, it was.

*

At least when Christoph left, he did not sneak off. He packed his bags in front of me and kissed us both goodbye. I didn't want to ask too many questions because he was in good spirits. Maybe this was what he needed. He would send for us soon and in the meantime... This was the missing part of Christoph's plan. He didn't consider what would become of us. Any normal wife would have asked for some guarantees. All I got was his aunt's address and a promise that he would write. He had always been a good letter-writer, hadn't he?

Usually, Christoph gave me the housekeeping money week to week. That day in October, he left me with an extra one hundred francs, and said I should talk to the housekeeper about getting my hours back at the hotel. I knew that my earnings wouldn't pay for our apartment, never mind the cost of a day mother for Ruedi, if I could even find such a person. I knew I was in big trouble, but there was no point in arguing. I let him go.

From that point on, one pressure was replaced by another. I no longer had to fear Christoph's moods, but I was filled with a different kind of dread. If I could not manage alone with Ruedi, I would lose him, as sure as night follows day.

I did not want to draw attention to my situation, a young woman with broken French and a babe in arms. So I had to solve my problem during Ruedi's naps before the money ran out. When he fell asleep in my arms after a feed, I would gently place him in the playpen where he would be safe if he woke. And I would run, run from one end of the town to the other, looking for solutions.

Depending on the time of day, I would use my time to ring on doorbells, asking for a cheaper room to rent. Late at night I would beg at the back doors of restaurants for leftover food. I tried all the women I had met in work, to see if anyone knew of a child-minder. I asked for my old job back and told the boss I was sending the baby to my parents in the country. If she knew about Christoph, she didn't let on.

This was new to me. I was not used to dealing with people directly, talking about money, making deals and making decisions. But my efforts paid off and within a few weeks I had the pieces in place –

cheap rent, a cheap day mother from Italy called Bettina who looked after half a dozen children of the hotel workers, and enough cleaning hours to pay for the basics.

November came and went and I was facing into Christmas and New Year with everything so delicately balanced I was terrified of the slightest misfortune that would bring everything crashing down. I was right to be frightened.

It started with Ruedi being listless one morning. His eyes were glassy and he showed little interest in his cereal. He just wanted to go back to sleep. But I needed to get to work and I packed him up in all his layers and carried him over to Bettina's place as usual. Just as I turned into her street, I shifted Ruedi from one hip to the other and noticed he hadn't just been resting against my shoulder, he was unconscious. All colour had drained from his face and his lips were blue. I thought my baby was dying.

There was no time to think or even scream, all I could do was run to Bettina. I hammered on her door and she understood from my panic rather than my garbled explanation that it was an emergency. I thank God every day that this good woman knew what to do. She pulled us into her bedroom by the front door and laid Ruedi on the bed. Immediately she stripped him and asked me to fill the bowl by the handbasin with water.

She called to her husband to bring vinegar. 'Now!' she shouted in Italian. While I looked on in dumb shock, she doused cotton socks with vinegar and wrapped them around Ruedi's feet. She kept applying a wet cloth all over his naked body, rolling him on his side to do his back. His colour and breathing gradually returned to normal and he started to cry.

She let me stay in her room for the rest of the morning, keeping vigil over Ruedi and encouraging him to drink. I was distraught. The tears of guilt and fear would not stop. Why had I not paid more attention to him this morning? How did I miss the fever and wrap him in so many thick layers?

I didn't want to leave. I was afraid to get him dressed in his winter clothes again. But Bettina had done her bit and did not want to be under further obligation. So I packed up and rushed back to our room as fast as I could.

My child was my life. Our home was a little love factory. I was afraid to take him out into the cold again. For two days and nights I watched him and did my best to calm his fever when it spiked every few hours. The only time I went out was to dash to the doctor's and back to request a home visit. He came and reassured me there was no sign of anything serious, I should continue doing as I was doing. As he stood at the door, he looked around our room with a sympathetic eye and shook his head, but he left with a week's worth of money nonetheless.

A week went by, and I missed my shifts at the hotel. The town was decorated with Christmas lanterns and garlands. People went around in groups, on their way to celebrations. My job and Bettina's help were gone. I went back to begging from the restaurants. One restaurant manager asked for something in return and we grappled silently inside the doorway among the crates of fruit and vegetables. Ruedi and I had meat in our Christmas stew.

I ran out of money and I ran out of ideas. There had not been a single letter from London, not even a Christmas message. My begging letter to Christoph's brother, Ruedi's godfather, was also ignored. Ruedi was happy having me to himself all day. He got one or two colds, but nothing as bad as before. He loved his food and he was growing. In desperation one night, I went down to the park on the lakeshore and sat waiting in the cold until a man stopped and spoke to me.

'Waiting for someone?' he said.

I looked at his shoes, shining in the lamplight, the sharp crease of his trousers. His coat was thick and warm-looking.

'Maybe,' I said. Under his hat, his face was in shadow.

'I could keep you company.'

I risked eye contact. There was no sign of danger in his face, just greed. The park was beautiful in the daylight. We walked towards the darkest corner.

'Open your coat,' he said. I had told myself I would do hand jobs only, but the logic hit me that the more I did now, the less often I would have to return.

'Five for the breasts, ten for my hands and twenty for my mouth,' I said.

'Shall we call it thirty for all three?'

All the time I was with him, I shivered uncontrollably. But I saw it through and walked home with enough money for another week. You can get used to anything.

The one thing I couldn't do was go to the authorities. I had not registered my change of address and I didn't know if they were aware that Christoph had left Montreux. I was trying to survive as a ghost. Plenty had done it before me.

Then, one day, Bettina came to see me. Ruedi went straight to her which made me glad and sad at the same time. He had obviously been happy with her. I made her tea while she watched him demonstrate his crawling and pulling up. It was honestly as if he was showing off to her, constantly looking over his shoulder for praise. I had to smile.

'He is doing very well, Esther. Yes, you are a clever, strong boy. I can see that!' Ruedi gave one of his delighted smiles.

'He's nine months now and sleeps through the night. And he loves his food. He's a good boy.'

'Yes, and you are a good mother. Brava!'

My cheeks warmed. It was the first time anyone had said those words to me. I kept busy with the milk and sugar, but when I was ready to look at Bettina again, her expression had changed. There was sympathy in her face, but also discomfort. I felt a shift in the room, the realisation that this was not a social visit.

'I have something difficult to say to you.' She glanced quickly at Ruedi, who was occupied with his blocks. Not that he could understand a word. 'So I will just say it straight.'

I replaced my cup on the table and my hands dropped to my lap.

'Esther, I am so sorry. What happened with Christoph, the baby's fever, everything.'

'Just say it, please.' My voice sounded foreign to me, dull and defeated.

'You have been seen. Different people are talking about you. They say you have an immoral lifestyle, that you are begging and also meeting men in the park. They never see you with the baby. "Who is caring for the baby?" they say.'

At first I held my breath, but then it broke through in jagged, wounded gasps. It was the effort not to cry. Bettina spoke some more about regretting she had not come earlier. She understood why I could not leave the baby after his sickness.

'You should go, soon, before anyone acts. Go to your parents, or Christoph's parents. Take some time to get your life in order. They can force Christoph to send money. I think Montreux is no longer safe for you.'

I will never forget the mixture of nausea and horror she left me with. As if cockroaches were crawling all over my skin. I had thought I was invisible, alone in my misery, but this was a small town and their eyes had been on me all the time. People knew I was in desperate straits, and they were just watching and waiting. For what?

I took Bettina's warning seriously. It was time to move on. But where on earth could I go? The Home was out of the question. I had only three addresses: the family I had worked for, Christoph's aunt's place and the last place my parents had lived. There was so little chance of them still being there, I had to reluctantly rule that one out. I was too ashamed to visit the family and understood they would have no reason to support me. So that left Christoph's aunt, who at least had a blood tie to Ruedi. And she had sent a knitted hat for the baby's christening. That said something, I hoped.

I didn't know much about her, but she had been kind enough to take her sister in. I imagined her as a capable woman with lots of children and grand-children, running a big farmhouse. She might have room for one more small person, give me enough time to get settled somewhere else. Maybe a factory job this time. How slim the chances were that I could make a life for us both. The walls of the small room seemed to lean in towards me. I looked at Ruedi's sleeping face for a long time until I felt calm again. And then I started to pack.

Ruedi's things took up most of the space in the backpack. For myself I took only the clothes I was wearing and some underwear. Christoph had left our family booklet so I could show that if anyone asked for my papers. It was a good thing he married me.

I wished I had a pram to lay him in and pile up more belongings, but that was a luxury Christoph had decided we could do without. I packed some bread and cheese and apple puree, our usual meal, and hoped my money would cover the train ticket to Fribourg.

I had made it to February. Just over four months since Christoph left and every day had been a struggle. I was back to my skinny self. The proud curvy woman who had strolled along the promenade in a summer dress the year before had disappeared. Like a criminal, I stole out of our lodgings in the early morning dark. I walked carefully on the icy paths, weighed down front and back by all I owned in the world.

Christoph's aunt lived in the German-speaking part of canton Fribourg. The six o'clock train brought us to Lausanne. Then there was a half-hour wait and I had to go into the buffet to keep warm. We were terribly out of place among the early-morning business travellers and a group of students wearing funny hats who looked like they had been up all night. No other children. Who else would drag a child around at this time of day in winter? They were all still tucked up in bed with a fine breakfast to look forward to.

With the little money I had, there was no room for unnecessary expenses. When the waiter came over, I pretended I couldn't make up my mind and asked him to come back again. The next time he came I said I would wait until my friend arrived. His eyes narrowed, but he was not mean enough to kick me out – not yet. Ruedi was wide awake and I liberated him from his blanket and gave him a hunk of bread to chew on. One of the sleepy students was watching. I looked the other way, counting down the minutes on the wall clock.

'Would madame like to order now?'

The waiter's voice was laced with sarcasm. A memory of my mother came to me then, sharp as a knife. I knew this situation. People had spoken to her like this, while I had clung to her skirts. These were the sorts of people who always had it in for us.

I was filled with fresh determination. I wasn't going to slink away. Let him throw a mother and baby out of the café onto a cold platform in front of everyone.

'Merci, monsieur. I wait.' My tight smile forced him to retreat.

Twice more he approached me and twice more I defied him. The four students were openly staring now, and clapped and sang a silly song the final time I repelled the waiter. I was aware of the whole room looking, trying to figure out what was going on. That was enough. I wrapped us both up again as quickly as I could and left by the nearest door.

The cold was piercing on the platform so I scurried down to the grand entrance where we were at least out of the wind. When the train pulled in, I walked as far down the platform as I could to get away from anyone who might have seen me in the station buffet.

The next hour gave me some respite. I showed my ticket to the inspector when he came, but nobody else bothered me. If only the journey could have lasted forever, the two of us warm and safe and anonymous, not yet hungry. And the main thing – together.

A feeble kind of dawn was breaking as we approached Fribourg. The train passed a barracks and I saw the soldiers up and dressed, already drilling on the green. I had no idea how close the bus would take me to the house, but I feared I would not get far in the snow.

In the station, I found the bus ticket office and showed the man behind the counter the address I had for Christoph's aunt. He switched to Swiss German when he heard my accent and sold me a ticket for the right bus, which was not until ten o'clock.

My disappointment must have been obvious because his expression softened and he looked at me more keenly than before.

'Now you're not just going to go wandering off from that bus stop, are you? Make sure you phone ahead so someone will meet you off the bus.'

He was not convinced by my feeble, 'Yes, thank you.' Ruedi wriggled in my arms. He wanted to get down and explore.

'I mean it. If you can't get hold of your relatives before you leave the station, make sure you get out one stop earlier in the village and you can try the house from the post office. Will you do that?'

His kindness was unsettling. This man, about my father's age, was concerned for me and Ruedi. What must it be like to have people care for you in this way? How different life could be.

'Where is the nearest church?' I managed to ask. If he knew that I had just handed him almost my last franc, he might be less interested in my plight. People are more inclined to help those with small problems.

The idea of phoning the family was not bad. I found the nearest phone booth and set Ruedi down on the ground briefly while I leafed through the phone book. It was a confusing system with a different alphabetised list for each village. Ruedi was covering ground fast so I ran after him and hauled him back. I managed to block him with my legs until I found the number and memorised it. But I was too nervous to call and he was too restless. I decided to go to the church first, the only place I could think of where it would be safe for him to roam.

I walked down a wide avenue of shops and cafés, the workers inside getting ready for the day's customers. Just when I was ready to give up, I came upon a huge church with big columns stretching out on each side. Inside there was no service taking place and just a few solitary souls kneeling by different statues in the side aisles. If I had a prayer, it was that Ruedi would be quiet.

I chose a pew away from any candles and took off my bag. Ruedi sat on my lap for a minute, taking in the strange atmosphere and marvelling at the colours coming through the glass into the gloom. But his awe didn't last long and he was soon anxious to get moving.

For the next while, I let him go off crawling for a certain distance before going after him to scoop him up and set him down again at the starting point. When he got tired of that, I held his hands and let him walk between my legs. I remember he stayed still for a long time in front of a statue of Our Lady with baby Jesus in her arms. I lifted him up and watched his little face study the figures and then look back to me. Finally, he pointed and made an 'ah' sound. It was the first time he had pointed at something and I knew exactly what he was thinking. 'Yes,' I told him, 'just like you and me.'

On one of our laps of the church, I paused at the parish noticeboard. The Mass times for Sunday were written up and I had my own 'ah' moment. If the next day was the fifteenth, then today was my birthday. Standing in the Church of Christ the King in a strange town, I realised I was twenty-one years old.

How the time dragged waiting for the bus. I was forced to go into a café next to the church because Ruedi needed a change. His nappy had leaked and I had to wash his lower half in the handbasin and dress him in fresh underclothes. Afraid of being caught, I worked as quickly as I could. The waitress called after me as I left, annoyed that I had tricked my way in pretending to be a customer. She would be even more angry when she discovered the discarded nappy and clothes in her bin.

We ended up back at the station with an hour to spare. Eventually he fell asleep in my arms and I found a bench on the platform. The Ruedi part of me was warm, while the cold worked its way into the rest of my body. I ate some cheese and longed for a hot drink.

The fact that I was now twenty-one helped me to put together a plan. Until then I wasn't sure what I was going to ask these people for. Now it was obvious. I had forgotten about the one person who had some responsibility for me in the world, my guardian Herr Schneuwly. His office was not far away in Bern. I should have gone there years ago. He was the person who had information about me and now he could speak to me as an adult. He would have an address for my family. Perhaps they had tried to contact me. If I could just leave Ruedi for a day or two with Christoph's family and borrow the money for travel, I could go to Bern and find out everything. He might even be able to help me get a job. Herr Schneuwly would not turn me away empty-handed.

My legs were aching with the cold when I boarded the bus with my sleeping babe, but I was no longer the lost and confused girl who had arrived in Fribourg two hours before. I was an adult with a family somewhere out there and a freshly lit flame of hope in my heart.

*

The chiming of church bells calls me back to the present. I have wasted nearly an hour sitting on the windowsill. I must speak to Fräulein Vogelsang, if it isn't too late. I throw off the blanket, jump down and put my indoor shoes back on. Down all the flights to the first floor, I hardly touch the steps as I dash to her office. A strip of light comes from under the door and I take a minute to get my breath back.

'Come in,' she says in her businesslike way. Of course, she is expecting me.

'Hello, I'm glad I caught you.'

'Ah, you know whenever I sit down at this desk, I get stuck. Please, sit. How are you feeling?' She puts aside her papers and folds her hands together, officially in listening mode.

I always feel ill at ease sitting in front of a professional's desk. It reminds me of dark days. Despite everything Fräulein Vogelsang has done for me, I am aware of this gulf between us. The possibility that she might be judging me, or worse, pitying me, sets my teeth on edge. And the power she has to make my life better. It's strange to come face to face with that power; I can always see it much clearer than the person wielding it. They carry it lightly because they never feel its effects.

But she cares about me. In her own way, she cares. I give some useless answer about feeling confused.

'It's a pity you happened to be there at that moment. Makes me realise our admissions area is too public.'

Trust her to make everything about the hospital. I have to remind myself that this is my drama, not hers.

'Why were you on the desk and not Marie, I mean, Frau Zemp?'

'She's sick today and there was no one else who could come at such short notice. Anyway, I didn't mind missing the fuss about the vote. My women's group... well, never mind. So, you never got an answer to your letters from this woman from Mendenswil?'

'No.'

'I believe they are advised not to have contact with parents. For the good of the child.'

'For the good of the child. And isn't it good for the child to know his mother?'

'Maybe. But your reunion with your parents was not successful.'

'Sorry, Fräulein Vogelsang. That's something completely different. We don't need to talk everything through again. It is a legitimate wish to see my son who was taken without my consent. Those are your words to me.'

'Yes. I'm sorry, of course I agree it's a legitimate wish. I just wanted to help you see things from the foster mother's point of view. She is following the common advice. In any case, you cannot approach her here. I can't allow it. She has come for medical treatment.'

'But surely…? At least I can try to make a good impression.'

'No, Esther. I think you should avoid any contact with her during her stay.'

'I thought you were on my side.' The tunnel inside me opens up and I am falling down, down. I grip the sides of the chair to steady myself.

'I am on your side. If she were to complain about you, it would be very difficult for me to defend your job, and your room upstairs. Don't forget you have a special arrangement here. What about the plan?'

'The plan.' I stop myself from saying *To hell with the plan!* When I have enough experience here, Fräulein Vogelsang wants me to apply for a more senior cleaning job at the university where a cousin of hers works. Then she thinks I will be able to afford my own small apartment somewhere cheap, from where I can apply for return of custody. They need to see stability, a home, an income. She wants me to be patient. What she doesn't realise is what torment it is every day, not knowing how he is, or whether someone is being kind to him. She doesn't understand how much love I have for Ruedi and what it feels like to be blocked from giving it to him. My son is a love-starved child. Of all things, I never wanted him to know that pain.

'You've come a long way since we met.'

I hate when she mentions that time. When someone sees you at your lowest, you can never really trust them to forget.

'I don't even know if he remembers me.' In my worst imaginings, he does not want to know me anymore. He pushes me away.

She wants to say something, but hesitates and changes her mind. Fräulein Vogelsang would be happy to talk about plans and actions all day, but she hates to see any emotion. I brush the tears roughly from my cheeks.

'You know what I'm going to say.'

'Be patient.'

'Yes, keep doing what you're doing – the job, your choir practice, the walks, the reading I gave you. It might be dull, but there is a purpose.' On my days off, she has me down in the library looking up plants, or going for walks to collect them.

'What about you? Will you speak to her?'

Fräulein Vogelsang takes a long time to answer. She looks at a photo on her desk, the one of her brother and her together as children. Everything is so nicely arranged in the room. I wish I could live in a room like this, with paintings of the countryside and a rug with intricate patterns, made in Persia or somewhere like that. A beautiful design you could never think of yourself even if you tried for a hundred years. I always take great care cleaning this office.

'Here's what I will do.' She takes a deep breath, joins her hands together and rests her chin on them. 'I will introduce myself to Frau Sutter again and look in on her a couple of times while she's here. At the end of her stay – that's in about two weeks – I will speak to her and ask permission to visit her in the convalescent home.'

A surge of excitement rushes through my chest. I clench my hands in my lap.

'You're right. Now that she has been brought into your path, it does make sense to have that discussion about Ruedi. I will raise the issue of visits and I will vouch for you. Just not on hospital grounds.'

I am helpless. The sobs burst forth and I cover my face with my hands. After a minute or two, I am aware of Fräulein Vogelsang getting up and approaching me. She pats my shoulders. For her sake, I make the effort to master my emotions. But I can't speak. I stand up and take her hands in mine. We make brief eye contact and both nod. I leave her to get on with her work.

From her office, I go to the hospital chapel and offer up a prayer of thanks. In the privacy of the dark chapel I let my tears flow, and when they stop, allow the long-lost feeling of hope to fill my heart again.

*

I did make it to the farmhouse in Fribourg that day, a sleeping giant lying in a vast field of white. After the shock of our arrival, the welcome was warm enough, but it was conditional. The aunt gave me a week to get my affairs sorted, and she gave me the money for travel. She also wrote a letter to Christoph – a waste of time for all the good it did. The mother, Ruedi's grandmother, was in some kind of stupor. She did not react to us at all.

It pierced my heart to leave my baby with strangers, but I had to take this chance to make a life for us. The lawyer, Schneuwly, saw me without an appointment in a poky office above a shoe shop in Bern. He said he could not do much for me, with three hundred wards on his books. He did his best, though. He found out my parents' location and got me a temporary deserted wives' allowance. It might have been enough if everything had gone smoothly, but when does life go smoothly? Ruedi and I had three more years together before I lost him to the system. But the story of me and my son is not finished. It cannot be. Soon, the wait will be over. Soon.

Part IV

Beatrice

Beatrice gingerly removed her new glasses and placed them on the blotting pad. She rubbed the painful grooves behind her ears and winced. They were a foolish purchase; she should never have allowed herself to be persuaded by the handsome young optician.

The whole appeal of coming into work today was that it would distract her from fretting about the vote. But now instead she was worried about Esther Lappert – again.

Chance is a funny thing. If she hadn't been standing in for Marie Zemp, Beatrice might never have noticed the name of the patient. Without the address, she probably wouldn't have made the connection anyway. Well, now she knew. And Esther was all stirred up. It was unfortunate that she happened to be standing close by when the woman was checking in.

Yes, that's something she would see about changing straight away. There was no need for a patient to call out her address to a crowd of people when it is written on the letter she has just handed over. In future, Beatrice would tell the admissions people to point to the address and ask the patient to confirm it was correct. This detail was already entered on her list for Monday. Beatrice was a great believer in lists.

Had she said the right thing to Esther? She had to give her some hope to stop her from doing anything drastic. It was always difficult to strike the right note with her. That social gulf between them. Well, she couldn't do anything about that.

Ever since she had first met the young deserted wife through her work with the Hindelbank probation committee, she had felt compelled to help. Despite her reduced circumstances, there was something so dignified about the girl, as Beatrice thought of her. She wasn't like the other inmates with their sullen, disrespectful stares.

After that first meeting, Beatrice had looked more closely at Esther's file and read between the lines how desperately she had tried to keep hearth and home together in her years as a single mother. The downward spiral of theft and prostitution had been rapid – and brief. The price paid, very high.

Maman would laugh if she could see her now. And, knowing her, it would be a cruel laugh. She'd never had any time for Beatrice's bleeding heart.

'This one always has a dirty little creature to save,' she would tell visitors. Only now it wasn't a dehydrated hedgehog or a stunned bird; it was a woman with many years ahead of her, a woman who deserved a better life.

Beatrice was not sure Maman would have approved of her work with the Bern Women's Vote Association either. She could be very scathing about Swiss women. In her eyes, they were doing womanhood wrong – not feminine enough, not demanding enough. In her forty-five years in Switzerland, she never made a real Swiss friend. Couldn't even bear the sound of *Berndeutsch*. Always making comments about the clothes and the hair of the other mothers as soon as they were out of earshot, sometimes sooner. No wonder people steered clear of her.

The only reason I am here is because of you, she would say, looking at Beatrice and Gabriel with a sour expression. One could say the same thing in a loving way. Well, Maman had been no better than any other bourgeoise Swiss woman herself, had she? A doctor's wife obsessed with running a perfect home, giving ever more onerous instructions to a succession of maids. She dressed carefully every time she went out, even if it was only to go to the market or return a book to the library. She may have kept her figure, but she wasted her talents.

Beatrice glanced at the window and saw her reflection. Bad posture, *mon Dieu!* What on earth are you doing? she scolded herself. A sixty-one-year-old woman at her workplace on a Sunday evening thinking mean thoughts about her dead mother.

The clock on the wall showed almost a quarter to seven. And Gabriel was expecting her on the hour! She hated to keep anyone waiting, especially her own guest. She flung her coat over her shoulders and changed quickly into her outdoor shoes. Would her brother keep his promise to cook something fine in her little kitchen? Beatrice had skipped lunch in anticipation of a good dinner. For his sake, she hoped he hadn't forgotten.

On the tram on the way home, she scrutinised the faces of the other passengers, a handful of men as it happened. The result would be in by now, Beatrice knew. Did she see the smugness of victory written there, or a faint shadow of shame? More likely what she saw was indifference. But to think of it! Beatrice would cherish the experience if only she could vote, she was certain of that. At the last meeting, one of the women had brought in her husband's voting papers to show the group and Beatrice had inspected them longer than anyone else. Discarding the envelopes and information booklet, she had held the little slip of paper with the yes and no boxes. It looked so inconsequential. All you had to do was take a pen and put an X in the box of your choice. A sliver of power. Was it too much to hope for?

Gabriel would be the one to break the news to her. At least he would be kind. At the thought of Gabriel, the mild hunger pangs grew more insistent. She sat up straighter and clutched her bag a little tighter.

The tram trundled to a stop and she swung easily out of her seat and down the steps. She hated the way older women moved, either hesitant or lumbering, or both. There was no reason for it. Despite being in her seventh decade now – how shocking that sounds – she had no intention of adopting the mannerisms of an older woman. All it took was a little discipline – the morning exercises, lots of brisk walks. She stuck to her pact to walk to work three days a week, weather permitting; perfectly manageable with the right shoes.

Ah, she loved the little enclave of turn-of-the-century townhouses in her neighbourhood of Breitenrain. Close enough to her beloved botanical gardens and the Aare, with all the shops she needed and a settled place with not too many children. She made it from the tram stop to Schützenweg without meeting anyone she knew. The lights were on in every apartment. A pleasant feeling of welcome came over Beatrice, knowing she was approaching her own cosy home. It helped push away the thought that bad news might be awaiting her there. But the illusion faded the moment her hand touched the cold gate. It was time to face the truth.

She let herself in and climbed the stairs to the second floor. It was still an odd sight to see a pair of men's shoes on the mat outside her door. Marc had never visited her in Bern in all their years together. If together is the right word. Goodness, Gabriel was playing his jazz very loud.

Beatrice walked into a blaze of light, music, cigarette smoke and other, more appetising smells. All the doors in the narrow hallway were open – kitchen, bathroom, living room, bedroom, even the toilet door – and all the lights on. The music, reaching some kind of frenetic climax, was blasting from her record player in the sitting room and Gabriel was in the kitchen. She called out hello and went to change, closing doors, switching off lamps and turning down the music along the way.

A few minutes later she stood in the kitchen doorway, wearing a sweater and slacks. With a glass of wine in one hand and a cigarette hanging from his lips, Gabriel was humming and stirring a sauce on the hob. It was good to see him content in himself. She smiled and he looked up and tried to look upbeat. She knew when he was putting on a front.

'Ah, there she is. The hard worker! Come in. Pour yourself a glass of your best wine. Come, Trix.'

He set her up at the kitchen table with a glass and a lit cigarette, and turned off the gas ring and oven.

'Well.' His face was a portrait of concern.

'Well?' she answered.

'They are bastards. What can I say?'

She thought she had braced herself for this, but hope will always wriggle in, that treacherous friend. The disappointment burst open in her chest, a dark flower blossoming. 'Ah, so it's a no. Of course. I was expecting that. What percentage?'

'You haven't heard?' He puffed out his cheeks and widened his eyes to a comical degree. The air escaped in a little half-hearted puff. 'Sixty-seven per cent.'

Beatrice took a deep drag of her cigarette. 'Damn it.'

'But we will not let them ruin our dinner.' There was a pleading note in his voice.

'Not our dinner, other things.'

'No, Trix, not tears. Don't let it get to you!'

'I'm not crying. It's the smoke.'

Beatrice didn't like to dramatise, but it felt like a death. On her vote committee they'd been rushing around frantically like doctors trying to save a patient – leafleting, letter-writing, getting the best women in the country on the case, racking their brains for ideas. But the patient never had a chance. It was all for nothing.

She had been a late starter, only joining the committee in '57 after she'd heard the about the protest vote in Unterbäch. She couldn't read enough about it, scouring the newspapers for every account. How she admired the women in that mountain village who had gone to the voting station, acting against everything they had ever been taught. The men deserved credit, too, for giving their mothers, sisters and daughters their own ballot papers for the vote on making civil defence service mandatory for women. They also went against the grain. Not that the votes had been counted in the end, but what a magnificent signal it had been – to Swiss women and the world. Anyone could see that the system made no sense; the moment for change had surely come. Beatrice was part of a wave of new members who joined the Bern association then: teachers, housewives, secretaries, academics. They all came together lit by the same flame. Her sisters-in-arms, what would they do now?

Gabriel scanned the kitchen in agitation, as if there was something in the sink or the cupboards or the bin that would save her. He felt for her, she would grant him that. He might be the only one.

Like a man who has made an important discovery, he held up a finger and his face brightened. 'You need some air.' He jumped up and opened the window, stuck his head out and shouted, '*Merci pour rien, bande de cons!'* into the courtyard. No response from the citizens of Bern, holed up in their cosy apartments.

The kitchen was so small that Beatrice was able to pull him back in by the sweater without getting up. 'My God, stop it, you idiot. Don't disturb the savages.' Their mother's old term for the locals, it raised a half-smile on her lips. Gabriel straightened his collar and sweater in a pantomime of being affronted. She stretched her smile a little wider.

'It was the wrong approach, you see,' he took his seat again opposite her. 'Next time you don't ask, you take. You tell them, "You have had your chance for – what is it, six hundred years? Now we the women will be in charge for the next six hundred."'

But Beatrice didn't have any more smiles to offer. 'Next time, what next time? I think I have to accept that I will never have the vote. That is the country we live in. And I'm sick of talking about it, sick of the meetings and all the stupid circular arguments. The voters don't care what we do or say because of what it would mean to them to grant women the vote.'

'What would it mean?'

'It would mean they are not better than us anymore. They can't live without that delusion.'

'To the women of Switzerland' – Gabriel raised his glass – 'may they have their day. And their dinner! Now, you stay where you are.'

Beatrice put up no resistance and took a long sip of her wine. She leaned into her tiredness, and enjoyed a rare taste of laziness, as Gabriel set the table and retrieved dishes from the oven. Despite everything, it was nice to be waited on.

He served her first and then took a much larger helping for himself. They chimed '*bon appétit*' together and started to eat. The meal was simple but perfect. Fillets of perch baked in olive oil and lemon juice accompanied by potato gratin and green beans. And he had even made hollandaise sauce.

'It's delicious, thank you. Everything cooked to perfection.'

He patted himself on the shoulder at her words.

'So, sixty-seven per cent. Did any cantons vote yes?'

'At least Geneva and Vaud. Possibly one other in *Suisse Romande*, but none in German-speaking Switzerland. I'm afraid I turned off the radio quite quickly.'

'Shame on them.'

'What can I say, it's shit. Everyone I know said they were voting yes.'

'Not the most representative bunch.'

He considered the remark and let it pass. 'You know, Trix, you've had this fire in you about women's rights for as long as I can remember. Do you remember what the spark was?'

It was a good question, one she'd never pondered herself. She cast her mind back as he topped up their glasses. The upstairs neighbours began their washing-up.

'I don't know exactly, but it must have been early, because I remember I already had my antennae up when I studied that fresco in the parliament building. Do you know the one I'm talking about?'

'By Albert Welti, yes of course, in the Senate Chamber. All soft yellows and blues with accents of red.' He dabbed his fork in the air miming the action of painting.

'Yes, well, we did a project on it in the final year of primary school.' She smoothed her hand over the tabletop, imagining the painting, too, in the big heavy book they were all allowed to take home for one night.

'And?'

'You know there are five panels in the fresco depicting an open-air assembly?'

'*Die Landsgemeinde*, yes, I'm familiar with it. With the Alps in the background.'

'We children had to write an essay describing the scene, and we had to choose a detail from the huge display to copy. I drew three boys fighting. Much too difficult, I made a mess of it.'

'Art was never your forte. More gratin?' She let him pile more food on her plate.

'I remember it so clearly and I've seen it since. Welti painted a throng of men, gathered to discuss the matters of the day and to vote. The older or more important ones, like the clergy and maybe judges, are seated on special platforms. The others, at least a hundred men, are standing about in their waistcoats and cocked hats, and you can see them weighing up the arguments.'

'Beatrice, I know the painting.'

'All right, I'll get to the point. In that whole painting, there is only a handful of women. They're sitting on the ground, wearing traditional costumes, with children clinging to their skirts. They are just waiting. And I remember distinctly how pained I felt by the message in the picture, all the more so because it was not mentioned by anyone else, including the teacher. The women were on the outside, not even looking in. They were not concerned with the matters of the day any more than the children were.'

'Ah, I can see how that would have had an effect on you. Always worried about justice and fairness.'

'Yes, and once I discovered this fundamental unfairness in my world, it was revealed to me repeatedly every day of my life. As if a spell had been cast on me, I couldn't stop noticing it even if I wanted to. Even at home. I mean, remember the way Papi used to speak to Maman as if her daily tasks and requests were so trivial and boring? He belittled her.'

'I don't remember it that way.'

'Oh, and the way everyone behaved at our Vogelsang family gatherings. When did our aunts ever venture their opinion? I used to hate how the men sat for the duration of the party and filled the room with their voices, never fetched or served a single thing or moved from the spot to deal with interrupting children.'

'May I clear your plate?'

'Thank you. You were never like them.'

'Fate had other ideas for me.' He placed a chopping board and two large apples on the table. 'Here, you peel and I'll slice.'

Beatrice picked up a knife and started peeling. 'It was everywhere I looked growing up – and since then: the greater role versus the lesser role. It's no wonder I never got married. Swiss men just aren't evolved enough.'

'Present company excepted.'

'Dear Gäbu, you are all the more a treasure for that.' She handed him the first apple.

'Tell that to the local constabulary.'

'You're not in trouble again, are you?'

'No, nothing. Carry on with your speech. It's good.'

'Well, I'm no Iris von Roten, but I have my ideas.

There's all the domestic stuff – the way women are brought up to practically run a hotel for their men and consider that the height of achievement. But it's the invisibility of women that bothers me the most. Look in the newspapers, listen to the radio, the museums, the galleries, the shop signs, the *Bundeshaus* for goodness' sake! I'd almost prefer if I had never noticed and never cared, because my outrage has no effect. I would have saved myself a lot of bitterness.' She held up a single long spiral of apple peel.

'But it's 1959, goddammit!' said Gabriel. 'Are they not embarrassed?' He brought his fist down on the table, and the salt cellar jumped.

Beatrice shook her head sadly. 'Why should 1959 be any different to all the other years? The whole campaign has been nothing but fool's gold.' She pulled the chopping board closer and took over the apple-slicing. Gabriel seemed to find it calming to watch her.

Did she really wish she'd never cared and never got involved? Never worked on the brochure with Annemarie and Marthe? That was a masterpiece! It had been her idea to include quotes from important men who supported their cause. The excitement the day General Guisan's letter arrived with his endorsement for the campaign. How eloquently he wrote about justice and the common good. The most respected man in Switzerland, Annemarie had said, her eyes shining with delight as she held the letter over her head like a trophy, and they had danced, actually danced, around the table.

The apples were ready and Beatrice scooped up the stray pieces that had slipped off the board.

'Wait, did I thank you for cooking? Thank you, dear brother.'

'You're welcome, dear sister.' He got up and started hunting in her baking cupboard.

'I'm talking too much.'

'No, no.'

'I've hardly seen you since Thursday. You must have got in after midnight last night.'

'Do you have any cloves?' She rose and found the cloves for him, which he added to sliced apples in a saucepan along with a spoon of brown sugar and a knob of butter.

'I'm not used to eating so much in the evening.'

'Or drinking.' He filled her glass again. 'We have to find our consolations somewhere, don't we?'

'I always look forward to your visits, Gäbu. I'm glad there are still rich pickings at the house auctions here.'

'We should both be glad that the old Bernese families have a tendency to die out.'

'As well as a tendency to accumulate a lot of valuables.' She was proud that Gabriel had a good eye for paintings and cabinetwork. Her own apartment was furnished with some fine pieces he had found for her. 'So, everything's organised? Tell me about yesterday.'

'It was business and pleasure, as usual. Buying and selling all day at the antiques fair. Sold most of the pieces I brought with me, and got a very nice writing desk – Munich, 1820s. You'd love it, but I have a special client in mind for it. The truck is all packed up with fresh stock and ready for the drive back tomorrow.' He got up to stir the apples.

'And then, after an early dinner with the Zbinden brothers, I met the rest of the old gang, and we ended up in a jazz club in the Matte. You can still have a good time in Bern if you know where to go.'

'The only place I ever go in the evenings is to the committee meetings and the odd concert.'

'There must be a club you could join.'

'Don't worry, the meetings provide plenty of entertainment. Besides, I have my walkers' group. Just waiting for the first sign of spring.'

'How was work today?'

'It was fine. A steady flow of admissions from two o'clock. It's all very streamlined.' She reached out and took the cigarette from his fingers.

'I don't doubt it, with you in charge.'

'Yes, well, it's not complicated. But it was good to be at the coalface again, if only for half a day. It's good to be reminded that every patient has a face, their own circumstances, fears. I could really see the fear in some of them today. Depending on the procedure – I mean all the procedures are unpleasant – but some are very serious. And I had sort of forgotten that aspect of it. The person at the heart of it all.' She offered him his cigarette back.

'Finish it. You know, you would have made a good doctor.'

'Better check those apples.'

'Beatrice…'

'Is there a better smell in the world?'

'I mean it. It should have been you.'

'Oh please, not this subject. You accepted the university place. You wanted it, too.'

'No, Papi wanted it for me and I wanted to comply, but I was hopelessly unsuited to medicine. I should have been honest about that. Maybe then he would have given you a chance.'

'No, Gäbu. I had so little faith in myself at that age. I would have messed it up, too. It's so long ago now. Why bother with it? We've both done well.'

It was true. The hospital administration job was a good match for her. She had built up the position over twenty-five years, gradually taking over responsibilities from the various department heads who were too busy to mind. And she was proud of how smoothly everything functioned. She had the respect of all the doctors, the board, the staff. Her salary was generous, for a woman. Between that income and her share of the inheritance, she was comfortable and secure.

And Gabriel? He was setting out the dessert bowls and spoons. He still had a boyish air about him, or did she only think that because he was her little brother? His figure had never changed, no middle-aged spread for either of them – that discipline was part of Maman's legacy. He wore his hair a little long on top, slightly tousled, a bit like that Irish writer in Paris, what was his name? The brown still dominated the grey, unlike her own hair which had crossed over to grey before forty, causing her unending inconvenience with hair dyes. She supposed people might take him for an artist, which was perfectly acceptable for a man in his business.

He looked up at her and grinned. Aha, that was the secret to his boyishness! At the age of fifty-eight, Gabriel, boy of the new century, still took life lightly.

'Done well? Maybe not in the love department,' he said.

'What's that?'

'You said we've done well. But look at you and Marc, and me and my situation. Not exactly romantic dreams come true.'

'I think you've had too much of that wine, Gäbu. First you're talking about the studies you abandoned more than thirty years ago, and now love. Or are you trying to distract me?'

'No, I've just been thinking about those years a lot lately.'

'Your twenties?'

'Yes, they are crucial years. I mean, you lay down the tracks of your life, and then you're stuck on those tracks for a long time. It's so easy to get it wrong. Or so hard to get it right. I didn't see that clearly enough then.'

'You tried out your fair share of things.'

'Including the inside of a psychiatric clinic.'

'That was only for a short time. You were lost for a while. Nothing to be ashamed of.'

'I'm not ashamed.'

'Well, good.'

There was an awkward silence during which the distant rhythmic wail of a newborn baby penetrated the flat from two floors below. Where was this conversation leading? Who was supporting whom here? He seemed unsettled. She didn't like to see him like this. Having gloomy thoughts was her department.

Gabriel turned off the apples and served two helpings. 'Crème fraîche?'

'It's perfect just like this.'

They ate in silence. The first blow of the vote result was absorbed, but the bruise of disillusionment would take a long time to heal. She pictured her fellow campaigners sitting around the table in their customary seats in the upstairs room of the Krone, papers everywhere, Henriette typing away furiously as her cigarette burned itself out in the ashtray. That wonderful feeling of common purpose, week after week, year after year. But was it really all over?

Gabriel took the two bowls over to the sink and tried to balance them on top of a colander.

Beatrice stood up. 'Why don't you go into the sitting room and relax for a bit? I'll come in to you when I've cleared up.'

He sloped off with a guilty air. When Beatrice looked around at the mess in the kitchen, she almost called him back. Every pot and dish seemed to have been called into service for this meal. Just as she pushed up her sleeves, the phone rang.

In a few short strides, she reached the chair beside the phone table in the hall. She sat with both hands on her knees and took a slow breath, in and out, before picking up the receiver.

'Beatrice Vogelsang.'

'I'm not disturbing you?' It was dear Annemarie, the most hopeful and hard-working of them all, who desperately wanted a better future for her daughters. Her voice was different, heavy with defeat.

'No, I'm back home and just finished having dinner with Gabriel. Oh, Annemarie. Have you been talking to anyone?'

'Yes, everyone, including Gabriel.'

'Oh, he didn't say.'

'No, I told him not to bother you, that I would ring again after dinner.'

'And how are you feeling? Did you go to Marthe's house?'

'No, the bus connections on Sunday aren't great. Anyway, I couldn't face it, not today. I'm too sad, through and through. I didn't think it would hurt this much.'

'I know.'

'And you?'

'More angry than sad. Insulted. Does Marthe still want to go ahead with the post-mortem at the Krone tomorrow?'

'Yes, of course. You will come, won't you?'

'I will. I want to see you and the others. But I think this is the end of the road for me. Let the younger generation come and do their bit.'

'It's not over, Beatrice! There's a lot of talk among the teachers. We may have enough women to organise a strike. And if the other cantons follow...'

'A strike? I don't know. They'd use that against us. Quiet dignity is the best way.'

'To hell with quiet dignity. We should be weeping and screaming in the streets.' Her voice cracked.

'Women's tears never changed anything, Annemarie.' Beatrice's cheeks were wet. She could hear Annemarie crying softly. Where were the right words? 'I'm sorry for saying that. Of course we can cry, we should cry. This is a hard day.'

After she hung up, Beatrice shuffled back into the kitchen and set to work. The simple activity helped calm her thoughts. She had found some hopeful things to say in the end and Annemarie had assured her that she would be all right. At least she had her daughters at home to comfort her.

It was after half past eight by the time Beatrice had the kitchen back in order. She put on the kettle and joined Gabriel. He was perched on the edge of the sofa holding a porcelain figurine in his hands. Aimless piano music spooled into the room from the record player, not too loud, thankfully. His bedclothes were balled up and shoved down between the sofa and the armchair. The good sideboard was covered with his papers, cigarettes and knick-knacks. A small packing case for fragile pieces took up most of the coffee table. It was true what they said about guests and fish, three days should be the limit.

She sat down in the free armchair and sank into a trough of fatigue. The pinching pain behind her shoulder blade was there again. While Saturday was for shopping, washing and housework, Sunday was usually her day for proper relaxation. The mid-morning phone call from Marie's husband had come when she was in the bath and she'd had to yell at Gabriel to force him to get up and answer the phone. Marie had never missed a day through illness – what could she do but take her place?

Gabriel was having one of his moments, seemingly unaware that she was there. She often wondered if he had these lapses when he was in his shop, but he didn't like to talk about it, so she never pressed him on the subject. He must have lost some customers over the years. After a minute or two he woke from his trance and held the ornament out to her. It was actually two figures, a boy and girl at a pump with a broken water jug at their feet. The details were painted in blue on white china. The girl's little hands were held to her face in shock, the boy's head was bowed.

'It's sweet,' Beatrice said. She normally had no time for this sort of sentimental bauble, but this one was in a different class. So delicately crafted, it captured something, an emotion, a time, a place.

'You can keep it, Trix. It's not very valuable, people only want the very old Delft. But this one reminded me of us going to visit Banon as children.'

'Except we weren't wearing eighteenth-century clothes.'

'No, but remember we used to fetch water from the pump.'

'Yes, that's right, I do remember going to the pump. The thrill of filling buckets of water for Maman.'

'It reminded me of those times. Though I've no idea why she sent us to fetch water when the house had running water.'

'Don't you remember? We begged her to let us. Because we wanted to do everything the way she did when she was young. Or maybe that was just me. You always fell in faithfully with my schemes.'

Beatrice placed the porcelain ornament on an occasional table. In her mind's eye she could see the alcove at the side door of Maman's old stone house, where she and Marc usually took breakfast in the summer. Every colour was richer around the house in Banon, the food tasted better and the air was charged with the scent of flowers and insect noises. She always felt more intensely alive there, and not just because of Marc.

The kettle started to sing in the kitchen. 'Thank you, Gabriel, I like it. Tea?'

'If you don't mind, I'll pour myself a schnapps – from my own supply.'

Beatrice nodded and fetched a sherry glass for him from her glass cabinet. The noise of the kettle was becoming shriller and she quickened her pace to the kitchen.

As she prepared her lime blossom tea, she thought of the old kitchen in Banon where she would prepare tea for herself and Marc in the evenings. She avoided alcohol when they were together, in sympathy with him. They didn't need anything to enhance the atmosphere, they created their own mood. The build-up to their twice-yearly meetings was exquisite. No one else would understand their arrangement, except maybe Gabriel, who could appreciate unconventional love stories. But it worked.

She had been well into her forties when she met him. It was her first visit to Banon after the war, and he had come to replace the stained-glass window in the front door. He asked her if she wanted to keep the same design or think of something new.

The question led to a discussion about which flowers lent themselves best to stained glass and they ended up poring over a botanical book together at the kitchen table, looking first at big-petalled flowers and, ultimately, fruit trees. He accepted a glass of water, and she told him the house was for sale in case he might know of a buyer. He asked to be shown around and appraised everything with his intelligent brown eyes. He looked at her bed a little too long. She didn't want him to leave.

Marc was quite reserved and respectful on that visit, but she was sure she had read something in his warm glance and his stillness when close to her. She simmered with anticipation waiting for his return. Would he see a trace of her wanton fantasies when they looked at each other again?

On his second visit, he unveiled the finished pane and held it up to the window for her to appreciate the colours. She looked at the yellow of the lemons against the green leaves and the blue sky, but her gaze lingered on his hands and his arms; she ached to touch his skin. She stood close to him and touched the outlines of lead between the colours. It wasn't her imagination. He felt it, too. He set the pane down gently and turned towards her. Their story began.

She never would have dreamed that this quiet stranger would buy the house and that it would become the setting for the greatest romance of her life. Yet she didn't allow herself to visit too often because she wanted to sustain the longing which was the motor of their relationship. And because Marc had other women. That was something she had come to accept. Everything else in her life was lighter and easier than it used to be because she had her twice-yearly visits to look forward to.

When Beatrice came back into the sitting room with her little Russian tray, Gabriel was rewrapping and positioning the items in the packing case. She sipped her tea and admired the gift again, the statuette of the two children. She could picture Gabriel clearly as he had been at that age – hair sticking up like a yard brush, scuffed knees and his shirt untucked. He wanted a pet, any pet, but their parents said no because of the surgery downstairs in their villa. In response, Gabriel spent a lot of time planning and imagining the farm he would have when he grew up. He kept ever-growing lists of the animals he would have and made drawings of the layout. He practised down the end of the garden where he kept an imaginary menagerie, including a donkey called Hansi, two goats, two rabbits and a short-tempered goose.

'Do you remember Hansi?'

He looked at her blankly, his own reflections interrupted.

'Hansi the donkey? You can't have forgotten.'

Gabriel tilted his head back and gave a silent laugh. 'He was a good donkey, never gave me any trouble.'

'He kept the others in line, too.'

'Hansi ran a tight ship.'

'Ten is such a wonderful age.' Wasn't Esther's son ten years old? Esther only had a photograph taken of him when he was much younger. What was his life like on that farm? Did he have a fantasy about being a city doctor's son in a nice big house with hours free to play every day? Poor child, he would not even know there was such a life. In truth, Beatrice had never really thought about Ruedi before. She held her hands to her face, perturbed.

'What is it, Trix? You're not getting sentimental in your old age, are you?'

She could almost see the connections in her brain spinning and interlocking like the mechanism of a watch. 'Did we have a good childhood?'

'What a question!'

'Just tell me what you think.'

Gabriel crossed his legs and leaned back on the sofa. 'We did. Mother favoured me and Father favoured you. It was very fair. And we didn't want for material things – skiing in winter, the chalet in summer, your year in Montpellier and my year in Berlin. A good education, considering.'

'They did love us, didn't they?'

'In their own way, of course they did.'

Beatrice warmed her hands on her teacup and looked towards the family photos displayed in silver frames above her sideboard. She knew them all by heart – studio portraits, picnics, mountain hikes, celebrations.

'Did I ever tell you about the young woman at work, the cleaner whose child is in care?'

Gabriel frowned and rubbed his face. 'Is that the one you helped after she was in prison?'

'Yes. She's suffered a lot. Like most of the women in Hindelbank, she was really there because of poverty. She was on her own with her baby and she couldn't make ends meet.'

'That's sad in her case, but personal responsibility comes into it, too.'

Beatrice's free hand clenched the arm rest. 'That's what people think. It's what I used to think. But really, it's money. Switzerland is a very cold place for a woman trying to raise a child without family support.'

'It's not that warm a place for the likes of me either.'

'So you can empathise.'

'Are you trying to suggest that I'm the same as a common criminal?' He shoved the sheets out of sight as if his own mess was suddenly intolerable.

'I'm not saying anything about you, Gabriel, no need to be so touchy. I'm trying to tell you about Esther and her son Ruedi.'

'Sorry, I don't mean to be touchy, but it's a very difficult line to walk for a man of my nature. You don't understand the strain. I make careful choices about how and when and with whom...'

Beatrice flapped her hands as if shooing him away. 'Gabriel, I don't want to know. That's your business.'

'All right. You don't want to know. How careless of me to forget.' He crossed his arms and looked towards the plant in the corner.

'That's exactly it! We're all nursing our own grievances – you with your lifestyle and me with my women's rights – and we forget to look beyond that.'

'In what way?' He still wouldn't look at her.

'I mean, maybe I can't change the situation of women in Switzerland, or you will never be able to have a liaison in the open, but what can we do on a smaller scale? Can we change someone else's life for the better?'

'I feel like I'm back in the *Münster* on a Sunday listening to the pastor. What are you going on about?'

'OK, let's change the subject. Let's talk about Papi's chalet.'

'No, that's a headache.'

'Yes, isn't it? I've left all the bother to you these last years.'

He gave a half-mollified shrug. 'It's true, there have been various things to sort out, endless things really. The roof, the damp, broken fences. Are you planning on using it this summer?'

'Maybe for a week or two, and you?'

'Maybe. But I want to go on a buying tour to Austria. I can't leave the shop for too long. The chalet is so beautiful in the summer, a bit too close to the village, but otherwise perfect.'

'We had a lot of happy times there. That's the only place Papi really relaxed. Back to the roots.'

He turned towards her again. 'And Maman was happiest in Banon. Seems like we shuttled between those two rural idylls for many years, chasing their memories. Odd when you think about it. But give me the city any day.'

'Have you had any offers on the place?'

His eyes narrowed to a shrewd degree and he tilted his head at her. 'Just the standing offer from Furter, which we agreed was laughable.'

'Indeed, and Papi would hate that family to get their hands on the place.'

'What are you getting at, Beatrice?'

'I'm having thoughts.'

'Could you be more specific?'

'You know, there was a piece in *The Bund* the other day about the oldest wooden house in Switzerland. Did you see it?'

'I don't get *The Bund*. Life's too short.'

'Ha, you're very droll. Well, this place is called the Nideröst House and it's in Schwyz. It was built in 1176. Can you imagine, a house still standing after so many centuries? And it doesn't look that different to the regular country houses you see everywhere.'

'Are we preparing for a general knowledge quiz?'

'I see you're no longer handling me with kid gloves. That's fine. As I was saying, Switzerland has a lot of Europe's oldest wooden houses, and the reason they have survived so long, according to the experts, is that people still live in them. Fewer wars and disasters helps, too, but the most important thing to keeping a house standing is for people to live in it, to open the windows in summer and keep the fire going in winter. Doesn't that make sense?'

'Yes, it's common sense.'

Beatrice sat back, dropped her hands onto her lap and gave a satisfied nod.

Gabriel yawned and stretched out his stockinged feet. 'I've an early start tomorrow. Should we close up shop?'

It had all become so clear in her mind, a fully formed idea. 'I'm not quite finished. Look, I have a proposal. The chalet belongs to us both and it lies empty eleven months of the year. Agreed? It's near the village which has a school and a hotel and quite a few businesses when you think about it.'

She could see the realisation dawning in his face. 'Is this about your protégée?'

'Yes. Only I haven't been protecting her very well. I've been urging patience and caution and compelling her to wait until she's in a better position to reclaim the boy. That's agony for her, and she's tried to tell me. But the truth is she will always struggle to put a roof over his head. At best she might only be able to afford one room, and that would go against her, given his age. She needs a secure home and we have an empty house.'

'But Trix, it's not that simple!'

'Why not? Why is it not that simple? I have poured my heart and soul into this doomed voting campaign, and I have nothing to show for it.' Her voice became thick with emotion and she paused to regain control. 'I am sick and tired of feeling helpless. I want to do something. I want to make a difference. We could make a difference.'

'She might not even agree to such a scheme.' He pressed his fingers to his temples.

'She might not. But he will be grown in five years and she will have missed her chance to love him. We don't have to stand by and do nothing.'

'And what about our hikes on the Weiss Alp?' Gabriel's voice had a petulant tone.

'We can hike it again when we're retired. That will be soon enough. Perhaps we could even stay there for short visits.'

'This is pie in the sky, sis. You can't just snap your fingers and reunite this mother and son. There are procedures, authorities. What will she live on?'

'She will have an address, that is the key. I'm sure she'd be able to get some work – cleaning, minding children, doing washing, something. She can say she's a widow.'

He leaned towards her and pointed. 'You're running away with yourself!'

Beatrice straightened her back and took a long breath through her nose. She would not let him unsettle her. 'It's an idea, one that could work. It's worth a try, surely you can see that. We can offer them a bridge to a better life. What if you could change the destiny of a young man like yourself? What if you could save him the hardship you've been through? You'd do it, wouldn't you?'

'You're a bit excited by the events of the day, you've had a glass of wine. Don't expect me to jump after you the moment you get a wild notion into your head. I'm not your little shadow anymore, following you around at the chalet tasting poison berries for you.'

'That only happened once.' Beatrice threw her eyes to heaven. 'But we had fun there, didn't we? Isn't it wonderful to imagine a child exploring those paths and lanes again, the back forest, the wooden bridge over the stream?'

'You're painting a pretty picture, but these people would not be holidaymakers. It would be a lot of work for them to live there and quite dull, too, I imagine. Anyway, I'd be very surprised if you still want to pursue this fantasy in the morning.'

Beatrice agreed it was time to get ready for bed. She didn't want to push the issue until she had thought it through some more and worked out better counter-arguments. But this wasn't pie in the sky as Gäbu had said. It was an action within their reach. It was something real and right. The average person would not be bothered with the effort of persuasion it would take to make it happen. She was not the average person.

She left Gabriel making up his bed on the sofa and got a head start in the bathroom. Beatrice tied a scarf around her hair and removed her make-up with cold cream. With the make-up gone and no hair to frame her face, she wasn't too pleased with her features nor the war zone under her eyes. When had her nose got so prominent? Silly to care. It was the overall effect that mattered, and the audience. Beatrice knew how to turn herself out well, a skill picked up from Maman. She fixed a few curlers in place.

Esther was still a beautiful young woman despite her troubles. It was surprising that she hadn't found a man to act as her protector. Probably they were all married, or too cowardly to take up with someone in her situation. Or Esther wasn't interested. Beatrice preferred that explanation.

Beatrice called goodnight through the door to Gabriel and retreated into her own bedroom. She put on her woollen bed jacket and bed socks, and took her notebook and ballpoint pen from the bedside table. She didn't keep a regular diary but always had a notebook on the go to put down her thoughts and plans, the odd poem. Today had to be recorded.

Voting Day, she wrote at the top of the page.

What was I looking forward to the most? Not the first rush of feeling, relief mixed with euphoria. That would have been sweet, but it was the recognition I imagined with such intense craving. I wanted them to say, this is your country, too. To have something solid in the hand.

When men say man-to-man, it means from one equal to another. To be included in that. Not always and only the second sex, the afterthought.

I thought I was angry before. Now I know how angry I am. As much as I wanted to taste victory, I wanted them to suffer defeat. Not everyone. But the ones who know full well what they are doing, and do it harder and meaner just because they can. To see those men and women exposed and humiliated, known as wrong forever more. That is a mob I would gladly have joined.

But there will be no mob or celebration. Tears must be wiped away and anger must be swallowed.

Gabriel coughed in the other room. The apartment would need a good airing in the morning.

She read back over her words, which seemed grandiose and self-pitying at the same time. Not a good mix. It was a good thing she wrote for her eyes only. She remembered meeting her old school friend Agnes for coffee and cake last year and making the mistake of straying into the subject of the women's vote. What a disaster that had been.

'It's all in your head,' Agnes had said. 'Whether the vote comes or not won't change our lives one bit. We all choose our path and learn to be content with it. Why can't you lot be content with everything you have and leave us housewives alone? My life is no picnic, but I wouldn't swap places with my Albert stuck behind a desk all day.'

She continued on with one trite saying after another – each to his own, live and let live. Beatrice realised that it wasn't that Agnes disliked her activism, she pitied her for it. Beatrice had slept badly for several nights after that encounter, composing and rephrasing the perfect speech that would get through to Agnes and her ilk.

She took up the pen again.

Recalling that meeting with Agnes last year. I could have had an Albert, too. At a given time, there were enough candidates hovering. I'm a good cook and I can listen. I could have washed large shirts and socks, positioned myself this way and that in bed once a week. But marriage always seemed to me the point of no return. Every story ends with marriage, but what comes after is little spoken about. It is lived out, though, everywhere you look. And I don't see the attraction.

She had forgotten children. She did not feel like writing about that. Beatrice looked around her bedroom, the glow from the cherrywood furniture so cosy in the lamplight. 'I am content,' she said aloud. Agnes was wrong about that.

Writing about marriage on voting day, how weak! I'm heartbroken, she thought. The emotion was suddenly too much, and she pressed a handkerchief to her eyes. Funny how saying it makes it so. Can you be content and heartbroken in the same bed on the same night? It seems you can.

Beatrice knew she was many things at once. She appreciated her blessings, but she was a restless soul. That was a blessing, too. It had pushed her out of home to get qualified in business administration. No simple secretarial course for her. It had pushed her to accept love but reject ties. It pushed her to walk twenty kilometres in one day for enjoyment.

And next, it would push her to secure a home for Esther and Ruedi, because she finally realised it was the right and best thing she could do now. It was the cure for everything she'd written on the page in front of her. Gabriel would see, this was no passing whim.

How did the saying go, *ein Mann der Tat*? Well, *eine Frau der Tat** sounded even better to her.

On the facing page, Beatrice began to write the first list of actions in her latest plan. The pen flowed easily over the page.

---

*A man of action/a woman of action

Epilogue

One year later

The final landmark was a rocky outcrop half covered in bushes. Peter took the next laneway on the right and they drove through a short tunnel of trees before the view opened up around them and they could see right across the sweep of the valley down to the shimmering lake.

Vreni took one last look at Fräulein Vogelsang's directions, folded the piece of paper and put it in her handbag. A flutter of nerves moved from her stomach to the top of her chest.

Margrit considered Fräulein Vogelsang to be too high and mighty, but that wasn't it, Vreni thought. Yes, she had a grand way of speaking, and just turned up whenever she pleased, always so smartly dressed. But Fräulein Vogelsang talked perfect sense, there was no denying that, and you couldn't help admiring her capability and confidence. Vreni had never met anyone like her. Indeed, Vreni was more nervous about meeting the mother. Would she be triumphant, resentful? Did she really want them to come? They were going to be an odd bunch this afternoon, that much was certain. Thank goodness Margrit had agreed to come.

There it was at last, a pretty wooden chalet on the traditional stone base, Ruedi's new home. Three figures stood in the yard, shielding their eyes from the early summer sunshine as they watched the car approach. The first thought that came to Vreni's mind was that this was a charmed place.

After a great deal of hand-shaking and remarks on what a fine day it was and how well everyone was looking, Peter explained that he had someone to see about a sow, got back into the car, and swung out of the yard.

The retreating noise of the engine left a noticeable lull. Vreni shook out her crumpled skirt to let some air at her legs. She tried not to stare at Fräulein Vogelsang's attire. Where had the chic lady gone? The older woman was wearing men's shorts and some kind of work boots, with a hat on a string hanging down her back that would not have looked out of place in a Western.

Ruedi, a half a head taller since the last time she'd seen him, had his eyes fixed on the ball-shaped parcel under Margrit's arm.

'Welcome,' Frau Lappert said again. She looked different, too, like a countrywoman. She'd lost that pinched, anxious look Vreni remembered from their previous meeting. 'You must be thirsty. I'll bring water. We just carried the table outside because the day is improving. Is it warm enough for you?'

'It's warm enough for anyone, I'm sure,' Fräulein Vogelsang said. 'Isn't the table lovely? Esther has done a wonderful job inside, too.'

It was lovely. Margrit admired the wild flowers and the tablecloth, and Frau Lappert blushed and said she had borrowed it from a neighbour, along with two chairs.

'The people here are very kind,' she said. 'I'll just get the water jug. Please, sit.' The visitors settled themselves around the table.

'And I've brought some wine,' Fräulein Vogelsang said. 'It's cooling in the stream.'

'There's a stream?' Margrit asked as Frau Lappert emerged from the house. She paused at the threshold and it struck Vreni that she looked as if she'd lived there all her life.

'Yes, just behind the house, Ruedi will show you around if you like. Will you get the wine, Ruedi? And when you come back, we'll have the cream cake.'

Vreni noticed a gleam in Margrit's eye. Did she feel she was being dismissed? She wasn't an entirely willing participant today. Ruedi waited, unsure. Margrit reached down to tap the parcel on the ground beside her chair.

'I have something afterwards for you, too,' she said and Ruedi's eyes widened. 'But first, the tour!' She took an apricot from a bowl on the table, jumped up and went off with Ruedi, looking rather boyish in her capri trousers. Vreni let out the breath she'd been holding. You never knew when Margrit would be sharp-tongued. When she was Margrit's age she'd already had two children, and yet she still thought of her daughter as a girl. If only she'd settle down with that nice young man from Lucerne. He was keen enough, that much was obvious.

With a jolt, Vreni realised it was her turn to say something. A common mistake of hers, she realised, letting her mind wander when she was in company. Ruedi was still in sight. 'He's really grown, and it's only been a few months.' She found her voice at last.

'Eight months.' Frau Lappert sat and filled the glasses.

'I'm glad to see you both together. And is he happy in school? Is he well?'

The younger woman smiled and the cornflowers on the table brought out the blue of her eyes. 'He's fine. He doesn't need help with his schoolwork and I think the other children have accepted him.' She glanced in the direction Ruedi had gone and looked down at her hands on the table. 'He calls me Mutter, not Mami. I understand. But some memories are coming back to him. He says he remembers the feeling of being with me but not places or moments. He didn't know my name was Esther. Imagine that.'

Vreni made a sympathetic humming noise. She hadn't been expecting this much honesty.

'He's an easy boy, easy to live with. He doesn't ask for anything. I wouldn't mind if he did.' Frau Lappert opened her hands in an appealing gesture and Vreni felt a deep chord of sympathy strike within her.

'Oh, he's a great boy, a credit to you.'

'Thank you.'

'Anyone can see it.'

'I mean, thank you for looking after him, and for helping with everything. I never got a chance to say that, and when I had the idea to invite you, Fräulein Vogelsang thought it was right and proper.'

Vreni placed her hand on her heart. 'Fräulein Vogelsang is the warrior here. No better person to deal with the authorities and lawyers and whatnot. I wouldn't have a hope.' They both looked at the older woman.

'You just have to act like them, as if the world belongs to you, too. It confuses them.' She gave a weary half-laugh. 'But seriously, we've still got a long way to go. There's so much I would like to see change and I'm not even sure we're going in the right direction. In the meantime, you inspire me, Esther.'

Frau Lappert, as Vreni still thought of her, shook her head briskly and reached to pin back a lock of hair that had come loose.

'Here you are,' Fräulein Vogelsang continued, 'going out to work early every morning, paying your way, making a home, raising your child. It's so admirable – and natural.' Vreni checked the buttons on her cardigan. She wished she could forget the young woman's letters.

Frau Lappert reached a hand to Fräulein Vogelsang and they looked at each other with affection. 'There was always a missing piece, Beatrice.' She nodded towards the house. 'And you were the one to notice that and to care.'

'Aha, she called me Beatrice, at last!' Fräulein Vogelsang laughed, but Vreni noticed the sparkle of tears in her eyes.

Frau Lappert rose and wagged her finger. 'Just this once! I'll get the cake.'

'Is that a vegetable garden I see?' Vreni asked her hostess, keen to give Fräulein Vogelsang a moment alone.

'Yes, feel free to have a look, and maybe call for the young ones. They should be able hear you from there.'

Vreni strolled over to the side of the house where a garden had been fenced off. Scents of sun-warmed grasses filled the air. The freshly watered garden was at the perfect point of neatness, with all the rows of young plants ready to grow wide and high – potatoes, lettuces, runner beans, cabbages, carrots. A better show than she had at home.

Margrit and Ruedi appeared one by one over a stile and came tripping towards her on the path. How happy it made Vreni to see her daughter relaxed.

'This place would nearly make me want to live in the country again, Mami – nearly, but not quite.' The clanging of cowbells drifted down from the upper meadows, making her laugh seem richer.

'Look at these fine seedlings,' Vreni said, and Margrit and Ruedi lingered with her.

'I was just telling Ruedi that I'm working for the Federal Railway now in Bern. I'm in charge of all the trains.' Another laugh. 'You should see your face, Ruedi. No, seriously, I work on the timetables. Maybe one day we'll be colleagues.'

Ruedi giggled, a childish sound Vreni hadn't heard from him before.

'You've done a great job here on the garden, Ruedi. I'm impressed.' Vreni patted him on the shoulder.

'We did it together,' he said, with a broad smile.

The pride in his voice was also new. Vreni suddenly felt like singing. To be part of something good in the world, how rare it was.

'So, tell me, what have we got here? I see potatoes.'

Ruedi began to talk in that sweet musical voice of his, telling Vreni and Margrit the names of all the good things they had sowed, all the good things that were to come.

Author's Note

The subject of the failed 1959 vote for women's suffrage first sparked my imagination when I interviewed one of the leading Swiss activists of the time, Marthe Gosteli (1917–2017), in her home in Bern. She spoke fondly of the wonderful women she had worked with, and left me with a vivid impression of the disappointment they had felt following the 'no' vote.

It's hard to believe that Swiss women were only granted the right to vote and the right to stand for election at federal level in 1971. Switzerland resisted the domino effect that saw most European countries introduce female suffrage in the first half of the twentieth century.

The problem lay in the direct democracy system that vested more power in voters than in parliament, and still does. Male voters had to approve a change to the constitution to grant women the right to vote. In a conservative and unequal society, hearts and minds were slow to change.

Voting Day takes place on 1 February 1959, when the referendum was rejected by a two-thirds majority. The impetus for the vote was an outcry about government plans to compel women to do a form of national service.

I think it's important to remember that for more than a century, Swiss suffragists tried valiantly to keep their demands on the agenda. They collected signatures, got their allies to submit parliamentary motions, organised protests and endless meetings, wrote books and articles, and even tried to make the legal argument that the masculine word for voter in the constitution – *Stimmbürger* – should be treated as gender-neutral.

In the end, an outside catalyst was needed to force the next, successful referendum in 1971 in the form of the European Convention on Human Rights. The convention dated from 1953 and by 1968 the Federal Council (the Swiss government) was keen to sign, just without accepting the clause concerning women's political rights.

This ridiculous prospect galvanised the upcoming, more radical generation of the women's movement, giving them enough fresh outrage to persuade the government to deliver a new referendum. Times were changing. Finally, the two-thirds majority against the women's vote twelve years before became a two-thirds majority in favour in 1971.

When I became a Swiss citizen in 2015, I gained the right to vote again after being disenfranchised for several years by emigration. One thing is certain, I'll never take voting for granted.

Clare O'Dea, Fribourg, 2022

Acknowledgements

The idea for this book was conceived on a forest walk two years ago, but the original inspiration comes from time spent translating the writings of the iconic Swiss feminist Iris von Roten, who presented a detailed cross-section of 1950s Swiss society in her seminal 1958 book *Frauen im Laufgitter* (*Women in the Playpen*).

I am grateful to the many older people who have opened up to me about their experiences of being marginalised in this era in Switzerland. Their honesty helped me to understand how people managed and how they felt in complex and challenging circumstances.

Special thanks to Yvar Riedo and Stefanie Schwaller of The Fundraising Company Fribourg, who supported the project from the beginning.

All the team at Fairlight Books have given me great encouragement. It was a pleasure to work with my editor Laura Shanahan. Thank you for your faith in the book.

The manuscript benefitted from the expert input of Barbara Traber, Corinne Verdan-Moser, Kim Hays, Sheila O'Higgins, Helen Baggot, Fred Kurer, Jennifer O'Dea, Peter Hanly, Anna Rusconi, Conor Kostick, Sarah Moore Fitzgerald and Thomas Schmid.

Warm thanks are due to my extended Swiss family, especially Paul, Ruth, Daniel and Isabel Zbinden. Míle buíochas to my Irish family: Helen, Ruth, my mother Máire, Thomas, Dirk, and all the cousins. Finally, heartfelt thanks to my most steadfast and patient supporters, my husband Thomas and my daughters Maeve, Ciara and Ashley.

Book club and writers' circle notes for the
Fairlight Moderns can be found at
www.fairlightmoderns.com

Share your thoughts about the
book with #VotingDayNovel

Also in the Fairlight Moderns series

POLIS LOIZOU

A Good Year

Rural Cyprus, 1925. Despo is recently married, heavily pregnant and deeply afraid. The twelve days of Christmas are beginning – the time when, according to local folklore, creatures known as kalikantzari come up from Hell to wreak havoc. Meanwhile, her husband Loukas has troubles of his own. Struggling with dreams and desires he doesn't understand, he finds himself irresistibly drawn to an Englishman, a newcomer to the island.

In a village wreathed in superstition, Despo and Loukas must protect themselves and their unborn child from ominous forces at play.

'With beautifully paced, rich prose, Loizou conjures the heady sights, sounds and smells of Cyprus, while exposing the horror that resides in her superstitions.'
—Lucie McKnight Hardy, author of
Water Shall Refuse Them

'A beautifully crafted meditation on the light and shade of the human psyche. Loizou explores one of the darkest of human fears – that of being ourselves.'
—Dan Coxon, author of
Only The Broken Remain and editor
of This Dreaming Isle

JT TORRES

Taking Flight

When Tito is a child, his grandmother teaches
him how to weave magic around the ones
you love in order to keep them close.

She is the master and he is the pupil, exasperating
Tito's put-upon mother who is usually the focus of
their mischief.

As Tito grows older and his grandmother's mind
becomes less sound, their games take a dangerous
turn. They both struggle with a particular spell, one
that creates an illusion of illness to draw in love.
But as the lines between magic and childish tales
blur, so too do those between fantasy and reality.

'Taking Flight *is a finely crafted,*
lyrical song of a book.'
—Amy Kurzweil, author of
Flying Couch: a graphic memoir

'*The exquisite writing of JT Torres is on full*
display in this deftly told and spellbinding tale.'
—Don Rearden, author of
The Raven's Gift

LOREE WESTRON

Missing Words

Postal worker Jenny's life is in the doldrums: her daughter all grown up and moving out, and her marriage falling apart. So, when a postcard from Australia marked 'insufficient address' lands on her sorting table, she does the unthinkable. On reading that the sender is begging the recipient for forgiveness and seeking reconciliation – and knowing it will never get delivered in time – she slips it up her sleeve and decides to deliver it herself.

Will Jenny be able to give the star-crossed lovers the happy ending she feels that, somehow, she's lost?

'A tender and wise understanding
of the human condition.'
—Gabrielle Kimm, author of *His Last Duchess*

'Loree Westron writes with a subtle
beauty that made me catch my breath.'
—Laura Pearson, author of
I Wanted You To Know

DEBBI VOISEY

Only About Love

There's no such thing as a perfect family. A perfect life. A perfect man.

Frank is proof of this. He's everyman and yet as unique as a fingerprint. With a wonderful wife and children who are the loves of his life, he couldn't ask for anything more. But time and time again he keeps risking it all.

In snapshots through time, *Only About Love* takes a sweeping loop around Frank's life as he navigates courtship, marriage, fatherhood and illness. Told through the perspectives of Frank and his family, this story is one of intense honesty about the things we do to those closest to us.

'*Debbi Voisey's* Only About Love *is a touching book about what it means to be human, flawed, and yet so full of love.*'
—Sophie van Llewyn, author of *Bottled Goods*

'*Gut-wrenching, heart-warming, playful with time, language and memory. A fine homage to love in all its guises, good and bad.*'
—Lisa Blower, author of
Pondweed